ORCHESTRA
of the
LOST STEPS

Shelley A. Leedahl

thistledown press

National Library of Canada Cataloguing in Publication

Leedahl, Shelley A. (Shelley Ann), 1963-
Orchestra of the lost steps / Shelley A. Leedahl.

ISBN 1-894345-67-3

I. Title.

PS8573.E3536O73 2004   C813'.54C2004-900865-X

Cover photograph *Calle 60, Mérida*, by Gerardo Montiel Klint
Author photo: Helen Herr

Cover and book design by J. Forrie
Typeset by Thistledown Press

Thistledown Press Ltd.
633 Main Street
Saskatoon, Saskatchewan, S7H 0J8
www.thistledown.sk.ca

Thistledown Press gratefully acknowledges the financial assistance of the Canada Council for the Arts, the Saskatchewan Arts Board, and the Government of Canada through the Book Publishing Industry Development Program for its publishing program.

ORCHESTRA
of the
LOST STEPS

Also by Shelley A. Leedahl

Talking Down The Northern Lights

Tell Me Everything

The Bone Talker

Riding Planet Earth

Sky Kickers

A Few Words For January

ACKNOWLEDGMENTS

I am grateful to the Saskatchewan Arts Board for financial assistance, to the Saskatchewan Artists/Writers Colony for the time and place, and, once again, to my friends at Thistledown Press for making it happen. Barbara Kuhne was my insightful editor and I thank her for seeing in these stories those things that I could not. *Gracias a* Gerardo Montiel Klint *por la fotografía de la portada*.

I am grateful to family and friends near and far for their unfailing support. Love and extra special thanks to Troy, Logan, and Taylor Rae for their patience, good humour, and for tea and sandwiches delivered, frequently and without complaint, directly to my desk.

The following stories have been previously published:

"Harm's Way" and "Baby Please Don't Go," in *Grain*, "Night Out," in *Canadian Author*, and "Wintering" in *Canadian Fiction Magazine*. "In the Land of Healing Waters," "Wintering," and "What Do You Think Your Life Means?" (as "Pushing Up"), were broadcast on CBC Radio Saskatchewan's *Gallery*.

"Night Out" was selected for *Canadian Author*'s Okanagan Short Story Award, judged by W. D. Valgardson, and a Saskatchewan Writers Guild Literary Award, judged by Dayv James-French. *Orchestra of the Lost Steps* was selected for a John V Hicks Manuscript Award, judged by Austin Clarke and Helen Humphreys.

CONTENTS

9   Harm's Way

26   Night Out

39   El Pitallal

54   Hitchcock's Women

71   Baby Please Don't Go

86   Somewhere in South America

101   Jeopardy

117   *Avenida Triste*

142   Orchestra of the Lost Steps

159   What Do You Think Your Life Means?

170   Toward the Moon

191   Wintering

205   In the Land of Healing Waters

For Jeanne-Marie de Moissac,
Nadine Penner and Lonnie Williams

IT WAS DECEMBER. I'D SUNG MY WAY FORWARD AND BACK through my Willie Nelson Christmas tape, a gift from my daughter who'd left Canadian winters behind to marry some guy with initials instead of a proper name. He had a half-assed magic show down in Branson, Missouri. I seen it once, or part of it. I left the moment he took up the saw to chop my sweet darling into quarters, like a beef.

I was halfway between down-on-my-luck, capital of Alberta and d'ya-know-anything-about-machines? Manitoba. I'd answered an ad for a farmhand in a rural newspaper. Seems the boss and his wife were going to be snowbirding down in Mesa and they needed someone to keep the cows and chickens fed until their return. Then there'd be seeding. After that, we'd see. Harvest was many potential problems away. I was two months owing on a by-the-month hotel room and the tight-assed manager had been riding me for a week.

"The gig is up, pal," is what he'd said. Gig, like I had some nightclub act or something. A magic show. So I stiffed him the rent, borrowed a TV and a full pack of smokes and asked the Buick if she knew which way we were headed. "Buddy," she said, "I believe we're pushing east."

I was on the doorstep to fifty and in a lifetime of dreaming I never thought I'd end up one of those unlucky sons-of-bitches who drinks alone in scummy bars on streets lined with pawnshops, army surplus stores and whores with faces you wouldn't wish on a dog. I've had some trouble in my life and I was at a crossroads right then. I was trying to get on track. It's like we all start life out with the same set of dice and I just kept rolling the wrong combinations.

So I had myself a destination and a map spread out on the seat beside me. It was torn on the fold lines and had a piece missing near Flin Flon, but I made out all right. There was a hockey bag of clothes in the back, my other boots, a sleeping bag, a huge, green-hooded Co-op coat — it floated down around my knees — that I'd picked up at the Sally Ann. The TV, a shovel, one of those dinky spare tires and a gas can barely took up half the trunk. I picked up a ham sandwich in Lloydminster and got a refill on my coffee.

It was night, and when I crossed the border into Saskatchewan the snow started to fall like fat little fireflies. Light stuff, the kind that lands on your eyelashes and sticks around for a bit if you let it. It did a dance in my headlights. There wasn't nobody on the highway except those bastards in semis who sneak up on your ass — BOOM! — and pass, double line or not. Half an hour later you're passing them and it starts all over again. I couldn't get nothing on the radio, and, like I said, I'd already been through my tape. I played with my headlights — bright, normal, bright again — honked out "Jingle Bells" on the horn.

I'd just passed one of those deer warning signs that they've got posted up all across the prairies. This one said deer for the next three miles. Jesus. As if a damned animal's going to know if it's five or seven. Anyways, I had my eyes peeled, just in case, when the snow picked up and started coming at me like gunfire. I suppose there'd be people looking out their windows on a night like this, so close to Christmas, thinking about how pretty it is, house all decorated up with tinsel and the like, family coming home for the holidays. That's one thing I've always been good at, imagining how the other half have it. It's not that I resent their happiness, their turkey with all the trimmings and Christmas cards looped across the walls. I had my shot at that, too, but it wasn't meant to be. Like I said, life's a game of craps. Somebody's gotta lose.

But I didn't like what was happening with the night. My left wiper kind of dragged behind the right one, and I wasn't sure both tail lights were up to snuff. One patch of black ice and a guy'd be in the ditch. Then what? You'd be freezing your bloody balls off, that's what. You're not supposed to leave the car, but if you leave it running the gas might get you. Damn near happened to me in Donnie's Thunderbird. He wasn't a friend, Donnie, just some guy whose phone number I kept crumpled up in my pocket for a few months. He knew a couple of women who weren't too hard to look at and we thought we'd all head out to Sylvan Lake for a peek at the water. Well me and Selena — the one Donnie forgot to mention had an artificial leg — were getting to know each other there in the back seat, and I was wondering how I'd deal with the leg, if it should come up, so to speak. Did she have a latch somewhere? Did the thing swing out? Turns out it didn't much matter. I got myself one doozy of a headache back there, and the pain kept getting worse. Before I knew it I was dizzier than all hell and spewing on my own lap. Freaking carbon monoxide poisoning: Donnie's muffler had a hole in it.

Anyway, the snow was driving at me now. My map had slid off the seat and to fish around for it could be suicide. If I stopped I might get rear-ended by a semi. I plowed through: speedometer said I was nudging fifty-five.

I finished off my coffee and was beginning to wish I had something to warm my hands with instead of my own thighs when I saw a smudge of light ahead. Then a whole row of single headlights stretched across the highway . . . a line of motorcycles coming straight for me through the snow. I blinked. Gone.

"Goddamn." I fumbled with my smokes. My hands were shaking so bad I couldn't get nothing lit. I'd seen ghosts before, once, a long time ago, but I was drinking hard back then, not stone cold sober. And I paid.

I finally got the smoke going and it was sweet, having that bead of light there, that atom of warmth. It was company. I tried the radio again but all I could find was a Billy Graham special, and even that crackled. I was digging around on the seat for my tape when I saw him. Ten, maybe fifteen minutes had passed since the apparition. I should have been ready, but I wasn't.

"What the . . . " I was already starting to slow when I saw him skid across the highway. His bike piled into the ditch and he was left lying there, flat out on the road, legs kicking like he was having some kind of fit. Most of me wanted to keep going, just drive right past this crazy ass, motorcycling in the middle of winter, in the middle of Saskatchewan, but it was the small part of me that won. I pulled on my hazards, stretched my toque down over my ears and parked the Buick on the shoulder.

"Hey, you okay?" I sort of crept toward him, in case he was missing half a face or something and I could turn around fast before I got a real good look. "You all right?" I felt like I'd been on a bender but it was just the snow, dancing all around us at strange angles.

The lump moaned. He was a big guy — a deuce, deuce and a half — and I slowly rolled him over, like a boulder. He had on one of those half helmets. A biker, face mostly hair, a thick ginger beard that must have kept him from freezing. But he didn't look good.

"Hey, we've got to get you some help," I said, pushing and pulling him to a sitting position. "Where does it hurt the most?"

"Arm," he said, then he puked a little in his beard, but there wasn't any blood. I had a better look at him then. His arm was sitting at the wrong angle. I'd broke my own arm once. Fell out of a tree. Mother had to keep it steady till we could get to town. She set it on a phone book and wrapped a scarf around the whole business.

"Okay, now. You're going to be okay. I got my car back there and we'll get you some help. Can you walk?" He was standing. A little wobbly, but I let him lean on me and we made it back.

"My bike," he said. "In the bag. Got to get — "

"Your bike is dust there, mister. What do you need? Want me to grab the keys or something?" I didn't know if that made a difference to anything, but I was trying to help him out. He looked pretty busted up. I got him in the passenger seat and we worked his helmet off together, me with both hands, him with his good one. He looked like a tough bastard, and I was thinking it was lucky for me he was hurt, but he was wearing a St. Christopher's medal. I could've made a joke about it not kicking in.

I'd left the Buick idling and started to pull back onto the highway. He grabbed my arm. "Stop, got to — "

I didn't like his arm holding me like that. I wouldn't have liked it in July and I sure as hell didn't like it with the snow and the roads and the dark, and him maybe bleeding somewhere inside all that leather. "I'm stopping," I said, pulling over again. "I'll get your bags."

They were huge, heavy saddle bags and they felt like two dead dogs as I hauled them into my back seat, but he seemed happier then, and I gave him a smoke, and before long his breathing was about right and we got around to talking.

"So where were you going? Edmonton?" I put the radio on low, even though it was still Billy Graham saving souls for a fee.

"Yeah."

His voice was different. I thought it was the pain.

"Where'd you start out from?" I asked.

"Montreal," he said, but he didn't say it like we would. He said it the French way, smooth like. A Frenchie, maybe running something up to his mates in the west. I hear they do some loony things, those Québécois bikers, but riding through the snow and all? That was screwed up. I couldn't get my head around it, but I wanted to keep it light.

"Well we'll get you fixed up here right away. There's farms all over the place. Should be one coming up any minute." That's what I told him, but I didn't really know.

He asked for another smoke then, and I passed one to him. He spent a long time looking out the window and I was glad for the silence — needed it to keep the Buick between the ditches — but I was afraid he might go unconscious on me. I decided to keep him talking. "How you feeling now?"

He didn't look at me. "Got anyting to drink? I'm so dry I could drink my own piss."

"Well now, no I don't have anything here but there's got to be something soon. Some gas station or small town where we can get ourselves a drink." I knew that was a stretch. It was 3:15 a.m. and this was Saskatchewan. There wouldn't be another all-night gas station until Saskatoon, a long way yet from wherever the hell we were. "Bet a beer would go down pretty good right now, hey?"

He mumbled something I didn't hear. I'd lost the feeling in my right foot and my left was starting to fade. I saw a haze ahead. A pair of lights as it got closer. A semi breezed past and I drove on faith through the snow it swirled up. "Jesus." Then there was another light ahead, a yard light. "Here we go now," I said, hoping to keep him conscious but calm.

It was a neat little place with the house snugged up close to the road. When I rapped on the door what sounded like a big mother of a dog on the other side got riled up enough to wake the dead. I hopped from foot to foot. A light went on above me and the face of a woman dragged from sleep appeared in the window.

"There's been an accident," I called through the glass. "We need your help." I could see that she wasn't too keen on unlocking the door to a strange man in a black toque. I've had my nose busted a few times and a woman I used to roll through the odd night with told me my eyes are a little too small for my face. That shouldn't have bugged me, but it did. The thing that still works is my smile, but this didn't seem like a time to use it.

"I'll phone the police," she called through the frosted window. "We'll get an ambulance." The dog was raising holy hell. She may have said more.

"It's not for me . . . a man in my car. I picked him up. He's hurt bad. Please . . . he could be dying."

She seemed to be looking past me. "Go get him then," she said, but she didn't unlock the door.

It was like trying to move a buffalo, getting him out of the car. "We're in luck, hey? We're getting some help. We'll have you fixed up in no time."

We must have made a strange pair hobbling through the snow to the doorstep. All the lights were on now. I rapped again, and this time the barking was further away, like the dog had been shut into a room at the back of the house.

The woman opened the door in her housecoat. "Bring him in," she said, holding the door open. "Right up these stairs."

The kitchen was bright as heaven might be and I could see into the front room. A boy of twelve or thirteen was on the phone.

"That's my son, James," the woman said, pulling a chair out for the biker. "You sit here and let me have a look. I'm a nurse."

"How 'bout that," I said.

The kettle was whistling on the stove. The nurse was helping the biker out of his jacket in slow motion. She looked at me. "Could you?"

I took the kettle off and poured the water into the waiting teapot. "Anything else I can do, Ma'am?"

"No, not yet. We've got to find out what's to be done." She leaned back and called to her son. "James?"

The boy seemed reluctant to come into the room. He was slight and fair, and I could see that he might have been the kind of kid who had asthma or got picked on in the schoolyard. "I tried again." Even his voice was only three-quarters there.

"Nothing?"

"Oooh . . . fuck." The biker moaned. Pain or not, I was embarrassed by his choice of words.

"Could you hold this, please?" She had him worked into a sling now, and was fastening it behind his neck.

My job was to hold up his ponytail. "Is the ambulance on its way?"

The nurse eyed her son, who shook his head. "Well that's just it," she said, now pulling off the black, square-toed boots the biker'd tramped across her pretty kitchen floor in. "The phones are out."

و

She made us chicken noodle soup and baloney sandwiches. The biker was beginning to get his strength back and I was hoping I could soon get out of there. I had a province to cross and the snow had already taken a good chunk out of my time. The nurse excused herself and disappeared. The boy eyed us from the edge of the room.

"Where's your fadder?" the biker asked.

I felt for the kid. It was like he'd been waiting for this. "Went to get my sister in North Battleford. She's in secretarial school. When the snow started coming down hard, they decided to stay."

"Ah, *oui?*" The man scratched his beard with his good hand. He had long fingernails. Yellowish. And they weren't smooth, like most folks' — his had lines in them, like corduroy. "My saddle bags . . . in da car. Bring em."

The boy shrugged, but he went to the closet and returned in a coat.

"Where are you going?" His mother had come back in jeans and a man's plaid shirt over a turtleneck sweater. She had all but the top button fastened. She'd brushed her hair and pulled it back with a band. No grey yet. I'm guessing she was in her early forties, but I've learned to err on the right side.

"Have to get something," her son said, "for him."

There was no doubting that *him* wasn't me. I'm not on the lean side of the scale myself, but compared to the biker I was inconsequential. A rabbit. I was hardly there. The woman looked from her son to the biker. Then she included me and I flashed her a sixty-dollar smile.

Her son was waiting. "Is that okay?"

"Sure," she said, sort of low like. "I'll keep trying the phones."

She turned and walked into the living room. I watched the biker watching her. I didn't like his eyes.

≈≈≈

"Your old man have anyting to drink in here?"

An hour had passed, maybe two. The boy was playing a video game in the front room. Maybe it was the sound that changed the big guy's mood — all that blasting and stuff. It freaking near drove me nuts.

"We don't drink," the nurse said, but I thought she was lying. I bet if I spied through their window on a dark, decent night I'd see them sitting around the table with the neighbours from down the road, rye on ice, a crib board and a bowl of chips parked between them.

"What's in der?" The biker pointed toward a cupboard with his good arm. He was walking now, stiffly, but he'd made it from the kitchen to the bathroom and back. He could have got out of his chair and checked.

"Pots and pans," the nurse said, quickly. "James, shut that off now. Try the phone again."

I knew she knew it was useless. No one would be out working on the lines in a blizzard like that, not at that hour, but I wanted to give her some hope. "You know, I don't think it's coming down as hard now. Maybe I could drop our friend here off at the hospital in town. How far did you say it was?" I stood up.

"Seventeen miles, but — "

"Assis-toi."

My French is pretty much limited to *bonjour* and the numbers up to ten, but I understood. The biker was unclasping a saddle bag. "Well, now," I said. "I don't think you need to — "

He pulled out a small zipped bag. "Open it," he ordered. I unzipped. Inside was a piece of rubber tubing. And crack, or heroin. I'd dabbled a bit in marijuana and mushrooms, but nothing hard. Nothing that could scramble your brains. He looked at the nurse. His fat, fleshy lips took up too much room on his face, despite the beard and mustache. "You're a nurse. You know what to do."

"No," she said, not so loudly that her son, one room away, would hear, but no-nonsense-like, as if to suggest there was not going to be that kind of trouble in *her* house. I bet she was a good nurse, too.

We listened to the clock tick. Five fifteen. Damned if I was going to make it to Manitoba.

"You'll do it," he said. His hand dove into his saddle bag, and sure as shit, he was packing. He set the handgun on the table. I've seen knives and brass knuckles — hell, one night I found myself at the wrong end of a broken beer bottle — but I'd never seen a piece before. It was black and long as his hand. It gleamed, and it couldn't have been more out of place against the blue-and-white checked tablecloth and salt and pepper shakers shaped like Holsteins.

She was a good nurse. She fixed him up.

I hoped he would sleep then. He closed his eyes, but anytime I stood he opened them again and put his hand on the gun. You never know how you'll react to a situation until you're there, in the thick of it. I was thinking that the woman must be thinking that this was the worst thing that ever happened to her. If she and her son survived this, she'd give her life over to God or adopt one of those starving kids on TV. I wanted her to know that it wasn't about her. It had nothing to do with her. It was my bad shit luck that had brought the whole thing on and she just got tangled up in it. I decided to tell my story.

"Once, when I was a younger man, I had a wife and a little girl and lived in a house not much different from this. We were only renting, but it was nice. We pretended, even talked about wallpaper and getting a little dog, which wasn't allowed. I was on a painting crew and it wasn't great but it was honest and steady."

The biker was watching me. One of his big mitts was still on the gun, but he seemed to lighten a little. I felt I could breathe.

"Sometimes on Fridays the foreman would call her quits early and the boys and I would all have a burger or Kentucky Fried, then go for a cool one. This was one of those days."

The boy crept in and sat beside his mother. She put her arm on his hand. Smart woman; I noticed she'd taken off her rings and slipped them onto the back of her saucer, where the biker couldn't see those diamonds shine. I was going to shut up then. The boy didn't need to hear this, but I was like a train in snow: couldn't see where I was going but there was no stopping now.

"So it was one of those early Fridays. February. I remembered that my wife had asked me to come home as soon as possible. She was putting in a roast and she knew I lost my appetite after too many beers."

The nurse poured coffee all around, like we were just a bunch of pals sitting down for a friendly chat.

"Jilly, our daughter, was in grade one. Anyway, I told the guys I couldn't join them and they were all calling me pussy-whipped and razzing me about it pretty good. So I went. Funny how close it seems. I remember what we talked about. The Toronto Maple Leafs and the Bruins. Ben's new 4 X 4. The hot little number that was setting pins at the bowling alley."

I seemed to have forgotten that there was a child and a woman in the room. It didn't matter. It was only words; no one was getting hurt. I went on.

"I was feeling good. Things were working out in my life. There was a chance I could scrape together enough cash for a down payment on a little house of our own. I'd come up out of nothing. A long way. Anyways, I seen that it was getting late and I'd better get home. We lived in the country, too. I wanted to beat my daughter home. I loved watching her get off the bus with her lunch pail swinging and braids flying, and I didn't often have the chance. I said so long to my buds and got into my truck."

"What kind of truck?" It was the boy. Maybe he was older than twelve. Maybe fourteen. I was surprised he had an interest in trucks.

"Ford pickup. Red. Where was I?"

"Going 'ome," the biker said. He was sitting at the corner of the table, on my left. He seemed to fade in and out of consciousness.

"Yeah, going home. To Caroline and Jilly. Well the streets were pretty thick with slush, and then it started to snow. I knew I'd had too much to drink but in fifteen minutes I'd be pulling into my own driveway. It wasn't no big deal. I turned onto the highway, south, and checked my watch. I'd have to step on it if I was going to beat Jilly home. The snow was coming down pretty good, not like tonight, but thick all the same. Suddenly this kid steps onto the road. I caught sight of him outta one eye, just a glance. I slammed on my brakes and did a 360 right there on the highway, but I didn't hit nothing. There was no kid."

Now the nurse had both hands on her son's. I knew if she saw me on the street she wouldn't have looked twice, but I had her then. She was mine.

"What 'appened?"

"Well I was pretty shook up but I got straightened out and started heading home again. I didn't like the way I felt. I'd never seen nothing like that . . . visions and shit . . . before. I stepped on her. All I wanted to do was get home."

The nurse was picking at her fingernails. Little bits of pink polish were flecking off, like dandruff. Her son had his eyes trained on me. The biker was smoking my last cigarette.

"I was going too fast. There was snow . . . I didn't realize how much I'd drank. The goddamn bus was stopped. I didn't see him. Seven-frickin'-years-old, crossing the road. Jesus."

The nurse gasped and slapped a hand over her mouth. Her son released a quiet whimper.

"You finished 'im?"

"I got seven years. One for each year of his life. Criminal negligence causing death. It's been a downward slide since then. You could say he finished me."

"You fucker," the biker said. Then he made something like a roar at me, peeling back those fleshy lips and showing his yellow teeth. I snapped back.

"I think you should go now. I've done what I can for you." The nurse seemed to be choosing her words like they was each worth a hundred bucks. "My husband . . . he'll be home soon. He won't like this."

We all knew that no one was coming through the storm before the sun herself took a shot at it. The biker growled. He was one ugly son of a bitch, with loony eyes, like pinballs the way he kept aiming them at the nurse, at me, the kid, the nurse again. His hand dropped to his crotch and he pulled at it. "Show me your tits."

Maybe she was pretending she didn't hear. Maybe she wasn't. "I — I need to use the washroom."

For a moment the biker held her there with his eyes, but then he gave a little wave and she got up. The boy started to get up, too.

"You, stay. Make me someting to eat. *Maintenant!*"

"It's okay, honey." The nurse hugged her boy's head. "There's eggs and you can put in some toast. I'll be right back." She held him a few seconds longer.

The boy put two slices of homemade in the toaster. He got the eggs crackling on the grill. We couldn't hear nothing but that and the dog howling behind a door again.

"What's da problem wit your dog?"

The boy shrugged. He was good at shrugging. The woman was taking a long time in the bathroom, but I hoped the biker hadn't noticed. I sensed she had something going on, and I was afraid. For all of us.

The boy set a plate of eggs and toast in front of the biker, who piled them up together into a kind of drippy sandwich. Bits of egg slopped onto his beard. The boy started whistling. I didn't like it. I could smell some kind of plan brewing, and I didn't know which side of it they put me on. The biker sopped up the last bit of egg and banged his cup on the table.

The boy poured more coffee. "Mind if I put some music on?" he asked, still polite like, but you could see that he was getting some balls on him now. He didn't wait for an answer. He reached above the fridge and turned on the transistor radio. More Christmas carols. He turned it up too loud.

The biker stretched his legs out in a V. "Where's your mudder?"

"The bathroom. Like she said. She's not feeling good, she — "

"You're lyin' — " He hobbled up onto his feet and lunged toward the boy with one hand ready to throttle the kid's scrawny neck. It'd be fast. He'd go down like a kitten or a bird.

I jumped. "Hey, now! Settle down there, mister. We don't need none of this here." He shoved me aside like I was nothing but a bag of wind and I stumbled against the table. Then there was this new sound. The door, snarling, and one black mother of a dog on the biker in a couple of leaps, lips stretched back and teeth like friggin' daggers.

"Son of a — ehhhh!" The shepherd had the biker by his bad arm. He wasn't letting go.

The nurse was there, shaking and looking small in her husband's shirt. A bloody scratch on her forehead, another on her knuckle. She must have punched through the bathroom window to come around the back of the house with the dog. "Move an inch and I'll blow your fucking head off." She held a shotgun to his temple. His eyes were doing weird things, zinging around in his skull.

I beat him to his gun.

We got him tied up with baling twine, and the sun rose. And the snow glistened. And a gas truck came out, and then there was the RCMP. It could have gone bad. It could have been a different story altogether. I made my slow way through the questioning, and then the snow, to my car. The nurse hugged me. Her boy shook my hand. A plow'd been out and the highway was driveable, but it'd be a Jesus long time before the snow was all cleared.

I never saw Manitoba until it was too late, but that was nothing sure anyway, like a kid's letter to Santa that don't even get mailed.

NIGHT OUT

THE GLASS ELEVATOR RIDES UP TWENTY-TWO FLOORS. CARS ON the street, smaller now, continue their manic pursuits. Lights blink out in high-rise offices, and the hungry river seduces another suicide from the bridge. Over there, the grand hotel. Three blocks back: city hall. An alderman has the new CPA dolphined over a desk. A bronze Mercedes pulls over for a gum-smacking girl. The driver says, "Call me Daddy." The run in her stockings will grow.

The elevator stops, doors stretch wide like a sideways grin.

Where it begins.

అయ్యయ్య

Carrie watches the elevator. "I can't believe we're doing this."

"Carrie, we're on the fast track to forty, neither of us has had a date since Jesus wore short pants — believe it." Mylene rubs her bare arms. She feels naked in the sleeveless blouse, a back-of-the-closet relic from her pre-Weight Watchers days.

"They'll never show. I know they'll never show," Carrie rattles on. "We should have suggested something else. Bowling, maybe. I play a mean five-pin."

Mylene surreptitiously consults a small mirror in her purse. She has lipstick on her teeth. Carrie should have told her. In the same situation, Mylene would have told Carrie. She would have told a stranger.

"You don't answer a personal ad and go bowling," she says.

Carries sighs. "Guess not. Hey, is that a mirrored wall or another room?"

They both look.

Everyone's staring because he's come in alone. He asks for a window seat — lies, and says a table for two. Maybe, if the gods are smiling, he'll need it. He senses eyeballs, like missiles, pinging off his girlish shoulders as he's led to a table near the wall-to-wall window, sketch pad tucked beneath his arm. He feels as if he's in an airplane, although he's never flown so he wouldn't know. There are so many things he's never done.

The waitress has small teeth and thick ankles. She believes the latter ruled her out as a member of the high school cheerleading squad, but the captain said it was because her voice didn't carry. Her hair billows around her face like cumulus clouds. Marilyn Munroe hair, he thinks. Marilyn in wind.

"What's yer fancy?" she asks, fluffing one of those clouds. She has an accent. Newfie, perhaps.

"Black Russian," he says, like it's nothing, like he leaves his little insurance office every day, dons a black turtleneck, rides a fishbowl elevator to the top of the world and drinks Black Russians. She knows, he thinks, she knows.

Mylene sips her Caesar. Runs her tongue along the salty rim. If she continues at this rate, she'll soon have consumed over triple her optional calories for the week. There goes the Lifetime Membership. Again.

"They'll never show," Carrie says.

෪෪෪෪

They look the picture of happiness. Arms chainlinked around each other's waists as they glide toward a table by the fireplace. They are like ice skaters on the Rideau Canal, or Torvill and Dean. "Here's to us," she sings, gazing past him to the bogus flames.

"Happy anniversary," he says flatly, reaching for the drink list. Earlier they'd spent eighty dollars on a meal they could not afford. Veal Oscar, chicken Cordon Bleu. She'd ragged on him for not swirling his wine.

"I've heard that a lot of couples get engaged up here," she says, groping for conversation.

They look to the sea of neon below, then up, to the stars and moon.

"Full moon," he says.

"It saw us coming," she says.

"What does *that* mean?"

That we're mad, she thinks. You're a werewolf and I've got the silver bullet. Go ahead, I dare you to make my day. "That we'll have a long, happy, uncannily healthy and prosperous life together. Our children will grow up to be morally responsible adults with nice haircuts and careers in the helping professions. In our mid-forties we'll be mortgage free and have a diverse range of interests, from growing kiwi on an arbour we've built with our own hands to breeding nonbarking, nonallergenic, nonshedding lap dogs for terminally ill children. Each Christmas we'll distribute handknit sweaters (we'll *both* learn, and love how it brings us together for reflective evenings while TV nature show hosts keep us informed about the latest endangered species we're campaigning for) to the ravaged men at the hostel — you never know, one of them could be Jesus. One day, when we're brushing up against sixty but — because we've kept fit with early morning kayaking and daily yoga routines — only look forty-five, a playground with nontoxic plastic equipment in primary colours and a catshit-free sandbox will be named in our honour. The mayor will present us with the key to the city, and — "

"I don't want a playground. I want a crescent."

They clink water glasses. She digs in her purse for a smoke.

The bitch! He's on the patch. Smoking could kill him. The big meal. The drink that will soon be trembling in his hand. He wants a cigarette more than he's ever wanted anything — even her, when they were seventeen and snuck away to the Lucky Star Motel to finally do it after all those months of pseudo-sex that made his brain swim and she loved him and he loved her back, oh so many full moons ago. Even more than that.

વ્યવ્ય

There are four of them, giddy, as if they've pulled one over on someone, like they're underage and got in on fake ID. Two girls, two guys. If someone were to accidentally fart it would keep them going all night. Of course they sink into the two leather couches separated by a low, rectangular table. The white candle glows between them like an omen.

"I thought the day would never end," the tall one, Sandra, begins. She's embarrassed by her height, is always on the lookout for low-heeled shoes that won't emphasize her size eleven feet. She frequents expensive shoe stores run by aging men who give off a certain unpleasant heat-and-odour combination. She holds her breath when they bend to slide her into styles that were hideous even during the last decade.

"Welfare day. Gotta hate 'em," says Brian, across from her. He emigrated from Alberta. He voted for Ralph Klein.

They order drinks. Strawberry margaritas for the women, beer for the men. They all work at the Royal Bank. The women will soon see the value of ordering beer over the high-priced margaritas. It's a cheaper drunk and just as effective.

"Well this was a dandy idea," Vance starts. He has very short hair and a nipple ring beneath his Hilfiger shirt. He looks a little like a British spy/playboy, if he does say so himself, and sometimes employs an English accent when talking to convenience store employees. He glances around the semi-dark room: other tables are filling up.

"What are they playing?" Gwen asks, tilting her head to the right. She's lost one earring but doesn't know it yet. They listen. The music is low, sexual.

"It's 'Smooth Operator.'" Brian prides himself on his musical knowledge. "By Sadie."

"I think it's pronounced Shar-day," Sandra corrects. She knows full well it's pronounced Shar-day. She's got the box set, but she doesn't want to embarrass Brian because he's fiercely attractive in a six-foot-four, paper-thin, loan-officer kind of way. She doesn't want to tell him that after work she goes home alone to her retro apartment, puts Sade on the stereo and imagines doing the wild thing with him in the vault.

"Great song," Vance says, and lifts his arm like a precocious schoolboy to flag the waiter. God, he'd look great in leather pants. The waiter, he's noticed, has noticed him, too.

ɛᴗɛᴗ

"Look, we've been here for an hour and Funny and Frivolous haven't walked in yet. I told you they wouldn't show."

"You're always so negative, Carrie. Even in high school you were such a bloody pessimist."

Carrie rolls her eyes. One contact lens slides to the corner and stays there. "Oh please," she whines, blinking like a strobe light at a junior high dance where young lovers mash their throbbing bodies together, woodies press against thighs and the dancers occasionally remember to shuffle as April Wine's lead singer warns that "Love Hurts."

"Besides, I've done this before," Mylene continues. "Remember?"

"Yep, old hat. That's what you are, Mylene. He looked like your dentist, took you to a slapstick comedy at the drive-in, didn't try anything, much to your dismay . . . "

"And we spent most of the night arguing about what colour the moon was." She laughs: a loud, infectious sound, one hundred percent real.

"Oh, for those high school days again," Carrie says.

"Perky tits."

"House parties."

"Twenty-eight-inch waists."

Mylene reflects.The waiter brings another Caesar."One New Year's Eve I kissed twenty-seven guys."

"No way."The drinks, the music and the smoke from the next table are taking effect. Carrie has stopped watching the door. "Tongue, every one?"

"Yep."

"Even Darwin Cheveldayoff? With those froggy eyes? He was at every party but no one ever kissed him."

"I did. I mean, it was just going to be an innocent peck but he stuck his tongue in my mouth and what was I supposed to do? It was actually kind of nice. And he had those spongy lips I wanted to suck right off his face."

"You're unbelievable."

"At least no one saw."

They order nachos. A plate arrives. They grab for the same one, the one with the most cheese. Mylene wins. She's not sure if she'll record this on the Weight Watchers food tracker stuck to her fridge beneath a Dairy Queen magnet. She checks her watch. Carrie bought it for her the year they turned thirty-five. Some gift. It doesn't have numerals on it, so she guesses the time. "I hate to admit it, but I think you might have been right. It doesn't look like they're coming."

Carrie laughs. Bits of nacho stick to her tongue.

"What's so funny?" Mylene thinks it's time to cut Carrie off. She never could handle her liquor.

"You said they're not coming, which means *we're* not coming either. Get it?" Carrie laughs loudly again, then slaps her hand across her mouth. Every few days she remembers that her parents never went the orthodontic route with her, even though a dentist advised them that a few years in braces would mean a lifetime of difference to her confidence. One front tooth overlaps the other. She thinks it will eventually move right overtop, and then she'll be able to open cans with one quick bite. It should make her very popular at parties, or incredibly useful if she's ever in a plane crash over the Arctic and no one has an opener for the canned goods.

"You're a real card, Care. A regular Roseanne Barr."

అ అ అ

No luck thus far, but the night, as they say, is young. He fingers the pencil. The sketch pad is flipped open on the table, the new page white and clean as hospital sheets. Lines take shape, become faces: a protruding nose here, small round glasses on that one. The waitress steps past, steps back.

"Another one, b'y?"

"Yep, this is from their Sergeant Pepper days. Which was your favourite album?"

"Don't know. They were before my time." She shimmies away with a swish-swish of her short black skirt.

He completes the sketch. Runs his hand through his gelled hair. It feels sticky. There are two women at the next table. He thrusts the sketch between them. "Do you know who this is?"

He gets Betty Boop stares.

"Is that Ghandi?" Carrie asks.

"That one's definitely Paul Newman," says Mylene.

"No, don't you see?" He pulls a vacant chair over to include himself. "That's John and George and Ringo and Paul. I always have a little trouble with Paul."

The women swap a look that says why-do-we-always-attract-the-biggest-losers-in-any-given-situation? His sketch falls into the ashtray and he whisks off the ashes. The world stops spinning. No one has anything to say.

❧❧❧

She lights another cigarette.

"I thought you were trying to quit."

"But I enjoy it so much." She inhales deeply, holds it in. Exhales. In his face.

"What have I done to you? You're so mean."

"Maybe you try too hard."

"How can I try too hard? I look back at our lives and try to figure out what I did along the way to make you hate me." If you knew about the affair with your cousin, then you'd have a reason, he thinks.

"You didn't do anything. I couldn't want for anything else." She looks out over the city. A police car tears down the avenue, lights flashing. She imagines the siren's high-pitched scream. "The comfortable duplex with just one coke-riddled addict renting next to us, three perfect children with only minor Attention Deficit Syndromes, adequate jobs in the meat-processing plant where every day we come home smelling like bacon — "

"What the hell do you want?"

"Fa fa," she says, imitating their two-year-old. "I have to pee." She pinches the cherry off her cigarette; there's still a good half left. "I'll be back."

❧❧❧

"Would you sleep with another woman for a million dollars?" Gwen asks Sandra. They are going around the table, playing this game.

"Yes . . . no . . . could I choose who it was?"

"No!"Vance and Brian interject.

"Well . . . "Sandra pauses for dramatic effect."I guess so."

"Brian, would you go to work naked for a day?"Vance asks. Sandra holds her breath. She wants him to say no.

"For how much?"

"Two hundred and fifty thousand."

"Shit yeah!"

Gwen picks the label off her beer, rolls it between her fingers and flicks it under the table. She suspects Vance. She kissed him once, after he'd driven her home from an unusually riotous staff party where one of the least likely tellers jumped into the pool in her white underwear. People snickered at her old-lady, hip-wader panties and sturdy, cross-your-heart bra. When Vance stopped in front of Gwen's house she leaned into him, kissed his neck, slurped his ear, searched out his tongue.

"I have to go," he said.

"Please."

They kissed a few moments longer. He was furtive, uncomfortable. "I'm going now," he said. She slammed the car door.

"Vance," she says now, "would you sleep with another man for ten thousand dollars?" The stakes have been dropping all night, but this is an all-time low.

What to say? Vance wonders. That I'd do it for a lot less? For nothing? That ten minutes ago I met the waiter in a washroom stall and we're hooking up later at my place?

"Yes."

Gwen gives Sandra's foot a nudge under the table.

"Not me, man," Brian says. "I wouldn't do it for any amount of money."

Sandra's heart leaps. Did he wink at her just now? This has to be the night, she thinks. The others come up with increasingly outrageous questions and dollar figures but she's lost in last Saturday, and Brian. The bank had recently renovated and there were filing cabinets to rearrange, new cubicles to make into their own. She, Vance, Brian and a few others went in to do the necessary shuffling. Brian in jeans and a T-shirt. She had never seen him in anything but sullen suits and cheerful ties before then. He was reaching for a file when his shirt came untucked, revealing three inches of skin. Beautiful.

"Sandra," Gwen asks. "Where were you just now?"

"Away," she says. Up, up and away.

જ⋅જ⋅જ

Long after last call, one and all ride the glass elevator back to the world of sirens and babysitters and bank line-ups.

Carrie and Mylene have been stood up. The ad *was* too good to be true, but for the moment it doesn't matter because they are laughing like the schoolgirls they will always be.

The Beatles artist, now there's one to watch out for. He waits in his car until the patrons have left and the staff file out of the building. The girl with the cloudy hair has exchanged stiletto heels for running shoes. She waves goodnight to the waiter and the bartenders.

"Hello," he says, coming up behind her, quickening his step to meet her rhythm. All those Black Russians have left him feeling a little like Rasputin.

"Hello," she returns, the word an exhalation. A warm wind whips her hair into her eyes. Marilyn Monroe, standing over the grate.

"I was wondering . . . "A carload of drunken teenagers speeds by. A bottle breaks on pavement.

"Yes, b'y, I'll bet you were."

Another distant siren. Her runners make no sound on the cement; his black boots click.

"Come, Black Russian." She shifts her purse to her other arm, curls her free arm in his. "Draw me a picture."

The anniversary couple strolls out into the night. The moon has a plan. "Still a full moon," the woman says, grabbing her husband's hand.

"That it is." He squeezes twice, fairly hard. Their unspoken signal for "I love you."

They walk to their practical sedan, car seat in the back, fingers still locked.

Gwen, Sandra, Brian and Vance face each other on the sidewalk.

"You guys want to do anything?" Gwen asks.

"I'm beat,"Vance mumbles. He follows up with an award-winning yawn. "I'll see you guys Monday." The waiter has directions, scribbled on a napkin. Vance tries not to sprint to his car.

"How about you two?" Gwen looks up, way up, at Sandra and Brian.

"I'll take a raincheck," Brian says.

"Me, too."

"What a drag," Gwen mutters, away from them, pumped and more than a little horny after all that talk of nakedness, money and threesomes. She discovers she has left her sunroof open. It rained.

"Where're you parked?" Brian asks Sandra.

"A block that way." She points north. "You?"

"Same."

They start down the street, jacket sleeves brushing. They come to Sandra's Geo. She wishes she had bought something roomier — she hates hunching in her own vehicle — but it's good on gas and a breeze to park.

"I had a lot of fun tonight," Brian says.

"Me, too."

He stares at the red neon sign flashing over her left shoulder: VIE AM SE F OD. "Do you really feel like going home? I've got some beer at my place."

She looks great in this light, he thinks. A bit like Meg Ryan in *When Harry Met Sally*, if Meg were put on a rack and stretched for a week or two. "We could watch a movie, listen to music."

She thinks he looks good enough to eat. She could fold him in half and devour him, like a deli ham on rye. "Tell you what . . . I'll swing by my place, grab some CDs."

"Sure. We'll listen to some music."

"Sadie," she says, shivering, though there's not a damn thing to make her cold.

DURING THE MIDDLE OF IT, SHE CONSIDERED THE STORY IT would make when they were safely back in Regina surrounded by friends, a Canadian Tire firelog ablaze in the hearth, their favourite Diana Krall CD at low volume. Of course Wayne would claim it was never that bad, he really wasn't afraid at all, and why did she have to fabricate every bloody thing into a front page crisis? Then their friends would shift in their seats, pick imaginary lint, ask how Danielle got along without them. "And hasn't it just been the warmest January on record?"

It was their fourth day in Puerto Vallarta and Andrea was climbing the walls. They'd spent their days at Playa Los Muertos, eyes fixed on the pulverizing surf and those fearless few who dared brave it. Wayne had dared, and was rewarded with something like whiplash after a particularly strong breaker — at least twice his six feet — pummelled his neck. Now he couldn't turn his head; even sitting on his beach towel required extraordinary effort. It was up to Andrea to deal with the relentless beach vendors — man, woman, child, troupe — who approached every two to three minutes, like labour contractions, she thought.

Do you want sunglasses? Cheap for you. You like a tattoo? Pretty braids for your hair? Braids? Certainly not at her age! The hawkers flogged ironwood turtles, silver jewellery pooled in suitcases like pirates' treasure, unidentified pastries that appeared varnished in sunlight, and skewered fish (they'd heard they were delicious but would make you sicker than a dog) along the scalding collar of beach.

Being friendly yet firm had taken its toll on Andrea. She knew the locals had to make a living but for the love of Jesus, could she not get five consecutive minutes of peace? They'd paid almost two thousand GD dollars in airfare for the privilege of being able to close their work-weary eyes to the lisp of surf and drink sunlight through the pores of their anemic skin, damn it.

She preferred the "Blue Chairs" section of beach, something she'd read about on an Internet discussion board. "I've never seen so many gays in my life," she'd whispered to Wayne, who perpetually trailed, head down to quell attention. But that was the fun of it. She *wanted* to see how this jovial, muscular, flamboyant-and-peacock-proud crew would react toward her equally well-constructed husband. She wanted to sit with them, break bread with them, cha cha and salsa in one of their clubs late at night. She desired adventure, come what may. But Wayne would have none of it. He ground his large, thick feet into the sand — they'd often made her think of pancakes — chin tucked as if intently searching for coins. He quickly netted the attention of a black man with well-oiled skin, pierced nipples and, Andrea noted, a sizeable package scooped up in a pink sac. The man made a sound like a cheap New Year's Eve noisemaker when Wayne passed. He followed them through the throngs — and thongs — for several uneasy minutes.

In the evenings they'd eaten late, stuffed themselves, really, and learned the Spanish word *satisfecho*. They drained countless bottles of Sol, Pacifico and Dos Equis — Andrea preferred Pacifico; Dos Equis won Wayne's allegiance — then stumbled back to their budget hotel room, where a sign in the tiny bathroom read: "Toilet paper in wastepaper basket only." Andrea kept forgetting, and Wayne, whose plumbing didn't jive with the flaming salsa, nachos and guacamole served at each meal, downright refused. She feared they'd bung up the hotel's entire system. Management would have to deal with it, and everyone would know, from the reticent Huichol Indian girl who made their beds (they'd been surprised about — and later, in the dead of the sweat-soaked night, grateful for — the single beds) to front desk Ramon, who'd lived in Germany and correctly identified Wayne's German roots (and ever after greeted him with clicking heels and the Heil Hitler salute).

Andrea'd awoken again — she was three for three — to the deafening conversation between the hotel's caged parrots. This after falling into an unlikely sleep against a background of car alarms, modified engines challenging land speed records and the catfight sounds of squealing tires.

It had been her idea to forego the expensive hotels near the beach, and — God forbid! — the all-inclusive resorts, and stay in Old (and much cheaper) Vallarta.

She propped her pillow and spread a map across her thighs. "I feel like exploring today. There's a town not far from here . . . Pitillal."

Wayne's right leg kicked, as if fending off a dreamland dog.

Andrea continued. "It's like a suburb or something. I've seen the name painted on bus windows. You can come . . . if you're up to it."

Wayne showed no signs of life. She grabbed his shoulder, gave it a firm shake.

"Jesus Christ, my neck." He winced and lost more colour in his cheeks.

"Sorry, I forgot." She swung her legs free of the sheets, scratching her bum when she stood. She'd frequented a tanning salon pre-Mexico and had burned her buttocks so badly she'd been unable to sit or wear anything except Wayne's sweatpants for a week. She was still a little tender — and bright pink where the skin had peeled — but it was the infernal itching that was really driving her.

"Oh, shite . . . the towels." The damp and sandy beach towels they'd hung in the windows were still damp and sandy. She snapped them off the shutters. "Damn this humidity."

"Yesterday you were praising it," Wayne said, his eyes opened now that the shutters were sprung and an unpleasant soup of light was pouring across his face. "You said it did great things for your hair."

Yes, there was that.

She loved that bus fare was only three pesos.

"Three pesos! What's that in Canadian?" she wondered aloud. Math baffled her; she didn't attempt conversions. They had the second last seat, on the right; she'd selected the back of the bus out of deference. Should the bus fill, as it was apt to, she would jump to give her seat to the nearest Mexican. Since arriving, she'd gone out of her way to be a nonstereotypical tourist. She'd seen too many already — Canadians and Americans with more money than manners or sense. They got pissed to the proverbial gills and treated the locals like fleas. One woman — a Texan, by accent — swatted a kid who'd been weaving through a restaurant queue with a cache of individual Chiclets. The child might have been four.

"I don't know. Maybe fifty cents." Wayne was making funny faces — pulling his lips apart, squashing his nose — at an ebony-eyed toddler who'd turned on her mother's lap. He loved little kids; Andrea did not. She was elated that their daughter, at thirteen, was miles down the *carretera* to independence.

"I read that Pitillal has a quaint town square. We'll get off there, at the plaza, or whatever it's called." She wrenched on the plexiglass window, hoping for another inch of air flow. It didn't budge.

They were climbing; the clay rooftops of Puerto Vallarta spread out like stepping stones. She searched for the landmark cathedral with its original crown-like steeple, but couldn't locate it. From up here the ocean seemed make-believe, a lone cruise ship like a toy boat in bathwater. They'd passed several small hospitals and an exorbitant number of autobody repair shops.

Everything seemed to be in a state of semi-repair: buildings, roads, cars, people. Generic, mid-sized dogs roamed freely — many the colour of wet sand — but they were adept at not getting killed by the erratic traffic.

"I had no idea this place was so big," Wayne was saying, now that his young friend had lost interest in his facial contortions. He'd cranked his torso around to face the window, bare knees scrunched against the seat in front. "How long before we get to this Pit-a, Pit-a . . . "

"Pitillal," she said. "Say it. Pea-tea-yell."

"Pea-tea-yell." He sometimes allowed her to get away with things like this — treating him like a child, or a student.

"Not long, I should think." How lovely, she imagined, to live up here in the hills with that sapphire bay sparkling below. Maybe we'll retire to a place like this after Danielle's graduated, the mortgage burned. She found herself thinking of retirement a lot lately, though it was still decades away. They'd be fit seventy-year-olds, the kind prominent on the covers of retirement magazines: lightly tanned and smiling with their real teeth, golf clubs balanced on shoulders. She saw bus tours in their future, a seniors' condominium complex, but not now. Now she wanted adventure.

"And how will we know when we're there?" Wayne asked.

Well. She hadn't thought about that. She unzipped her backpack for the tourist map and simultaneously surveyed the Mexican across the aisle: eyes closed, a gargantuan sack of peanuts balanced between his knees, body rocking as the road dipped and curved. Nice, she thought. The bus stopped to drop passengers, pick up more.

Andrea turned to the woman behind them and quickly took in her dark eyes. "Excuse me, *por favor*, do you know if we're almost in Pitillal?" She pointed to her map, limp with humidity and the perspiration from her hands. The woman stared at the map for five seconds, then said something in Spanglish which Andrea translated to mean, "I don't read maps."

"Oh, well, thanks. *Muchas gracias, señora.*" She turned, her face prickling.

Wayne nudged her in the ribs. "Smooth."

They took a sharp right and appeared to be on a major street, a boulevard of sorts. "Surely this is Pitillal now," she said, and looked for signs that might confirm her hope. *Nada.* Even the buildings that may have been hotels bore no identifying marks.

Someone whistled like a referee and the bus careened to the curb, letting six people off: three through the front door, three through the back. "This is weird," Andrea said. "I was sure it wasn't that far away."

The bus jolted forward again, and the little girl with black button eyes fell asleep on her mother's chest. They lurched on. Andrea felt her hair pasting to the nape of her neck. She was wearing a short sundress — too short for someone on the backstretch to middle-age, she supposed — thick socks and hiking boots. Danielle would *die* if she saw her. Danielle *died* no matter what Andrea wore. Her daughter'd made a pasttime out of ridiculing Andrea's wardrobe, especially anything with shoulder pads. "That look went out with 'Star Trek,' Mom."

Andrea's focus turned outward. They were in a residential section now; the streets were very narrow. "The real Mexico," she said, "no picturesque cobblestone streets up here." They passed a man in two different shoes leading a donkey, and she snapped a photo.

"You shouldn't do that," Wayne chastised. "It's very rude."

"Nobody saw." There'd been many Kodak moments she'd wanted to capture — the ancient, strolling musicians on the beach serenading a clutch of Canadian seniors; the woman squatting on the sidewalk, arthritic fingers twisted like pipe cleaners; a portly, white-haired Caucasion kissing a prepubescent Mexican in the Blue Chairs zone — but good Canadian common sense and Prairie manners had held her back.

"These houses are getting pretty shacky,"Wayne said.

How hadn't she noticed? They were still climbing, but they seemed to have left the businesses, the tightly packed streets.This was the boondocks. Homes were little more than lean-tos, rust-coloured chickens jerked around in the dirt among the tossed bottles, papers, tires, broken furniture and various automotive or machine parts.

The driver stopped again and a blind man felt his way up the steps, one hand on the shoulder of a woman whose face was rearranged: nose wedged offcentre, eyes not quite balanced, lower lip swelled to the size of a bulging pea pod. She sat in the second seat.The man continued on, dragging one hand along the tops of the seats, a denim-wrapped boom box cradled beneath his free arm.Two round holes were cut out for the speakers. He stood in the approximate middle of the bus, gripped the overhead handrail, pushed a boom box button and began to sing: a slow, mournful tune in which *corazon* was often repeated.

"Pretty good voice."Wayne was digging in his pocket, anticipating the man's ramble down the aisle for pesos. They'd experienced travelling serenaders before, but never blind ones.

Andrea felt compelled to clap, but no one else did so she — when in Rome — refrained. When the singer approached their seat, Wayne offered five pesos. "Here a peso, there a peso, everywhere a peso peso."

"Shhht. He's blind, not deaf," Andrea chided when he moved on. "Now who's being rude?"

The bus stopped sharply, pitching Andrea forward. The singer, his disfigured friend and six other passengers piled off. There was no one in front of them now.

Someone tapped Andrea's shoulder: a man in a blue striped T-shirt and dark sunglasses. When had the woman who didn't read maps leave the bus? Andrea shook her head. She was losing track of things.

"Excuse me," the man said. "Where are you going?"

"To Pitillal, the plaza. Have we . . . I'm afraid we've missed it."

The man's face broke into a luminescent smile and Andrea felt the knot in her stomach unravel. Friendly, *and* he spoke English.

"Yes, you did miss it. Back there, about fifteen minutes ago." He pointed out the back window.

Wayne sighed. He still couldn't turn around.

"Gosh, I didn't even realize," Andrea said.

"Listen, I'm a bus driver. You can get out with me at the bus station . . . I'll show you which bus to take back into town. *¿Está bien?*"

"*Bien, gracias.*" Andrea grinned at Wayne, and gave the thumbs up sign. Everything would work out.

❧❧❧

"Unbelievable," she said. "We're still climbing." They were a good distance above Pitillal now, and even further above Puerto Vallarta. "I haven't got a hot clue where we are."

They passed two pigs grazing in the ditch, then came upon another stretch of houses that begged paint and a miracle. Clothes and rags hung on lines between trees like banners for poverty. The bus rocked over impressive ruts. "Can you imagine this place in the rainy season?"

"Hell," Wayne said, quietly, "I'm having trouble getting my head around it now."

Another movement captured Andrea's eye. A Barbie doll-sized Virgin Mary was swinging back and forth below the driver's rearview mirror. Andrea noted a sign behind the busy icon. She guessed it meant, "Do not distract the driver." She lifted her bum and peeled the skirt away from her legs. Out the window, on her left, a young man in a long T-shirt was teasing a large white hound. The man was sitting on a slab of concrete, bare legs spread. He appeared to be trying to . . . for the love of God, no! He'd grabbed the dog's back legs and was pulling it toward his groin, positioning the struggling animal so he could . . . unthinkable. Andrea's breakfast rose to the back of her tongue; the acidity made her cough. Wayne squeezed her knee, twice, hard; he'd seen it, too.

The bus rounded another corner. "We get out here," the bus driver behind them said, apparently oblivious to the boy and the dog.

Andrea and Wayne followed the driver off. No bus station, Andrea noted.

Their Good Samaritan removed his sunglasses and clipped them onto his shirt. "My name is Luis."

"Mucho gusto," Andrea said. "I'm Andrea, and this is my husband, Wayne. We're Canadian."

They shook hands all around and began an inclined hike up the gravelled road. Wayne was trailing — what was new? She shoulderchecked and noted the clenched fists, his lips mouthing silent obscenities. It was very hot.

They approached a graveyard of trees. "Mango trees," Luis explained. "They used to bear fruit but the people got too greedy and now the trees are no good."

"Oh." Andrea listened to the crackle and crunch of minute stones beneath her boots. They were ideal for this hike, but she wished she'd been more practical about the dress. What had she been thinking? Of course she should have worn shorts.

An eyesore of rebar, bricks and boards had been left in a haphazard pile beside the road.

"You could build a house here, cheap," Luis said.

She intuited Wayne's mental response: *Yeah, real cheap*.

"This man is building for forty thousand."

In American, Canadian or pesos? Wayne wanted to know. The more they discussed the issue, the more confused the conversation became. Andrea just walked. Where were they going? There was nothing up here. No one to ever know where they were. No one would ever find them. She dug for her water. Warm as tea.

They continued their march. Andrea felt like Forrest Gump. Where would they end up? Luis and Wayne had abandoned the property discussion. The silence was something new, and not meditative. She must find something to talk about. She dug into her backpack and produced three photographs: their back yard after a dump of October snow; the yard in July — the chaotic splash of flowers like dabs of oil paint on canvas; and Danielle's school photo. A beauty, people said. Gorgeous. In this photo her long red hair was pulled back in a sophisticated style she rarely ever wore; it made her appear much older than she was.

Luis clucked at the snowy photograph and the summer garden. He snatched the photograph of Danielle from Andrea's fingers and stopped. *"Muy hermosa. How old?"*

"Thirteen," Wayne said. "Just turned."

"She looks older. She is a model?" He wolf-whistled and the sound seemed to hang in the air, then spread out over the hills and further, into the mountains and jungle. There were boa constrictors in there, and jaguars. Andrea'd read that on the Internet, too.

"Thank you," she said, reaching for the picture. Luis hung on.

"You must bring her to Mexico," he said, still ogling. "Many Canadians bring their children here for school."

Wayne gave a little laugh. A surprisingly girlish sound from such a large man, she thought. "I don't think so."

"I want to meet her. You are returning to Mexico?"

Andrea hardly gave the question a moment's thought. It'd be a frosty Friday in hell before she ever dragged Wayne back. "Three, maybe four years from now." She had to say something.

"So long," Luis whined, "and already I'm in love."

Good God, Andrea thought. As *if*! And he thinks we have money. He thinks we're rich. "Well, we have to save our money for a long time before we travel." She tweezed the photograph from his fingers and zipped it back into a compartment in her wallet. She reached for the refuge of Wayne's hand.

A large U of sweat had formed below her husband's collar. "So where's this bus station?"

"Right up there," Luis said, and sure enough, just ahead five dilapidated buses were parked in a field and about ten men were gathered beneath a *palapa* shade.

"That's the bus station?" Andrea tried not to sound like a damned bloody tourist, but this was too much. The blind man, the perv with the dog and now this. There were a few sentences spoken in Spanish, the words all smacked together so she couldn't understand a single one.

She and Wayne said *"Hola"* and Andrea sat precariously on the bench, a few feet from the closest man, who was wielding a large knife like one might use for gutting moose. Woodcarving, she noted. He's making something.

"Amigo, sit," Luis ordered.

"I'm good," Wayne said; Andrea thought he sounded snarky.

Oh, God. Her already short dress had crept up her thigh. She inched it toward her knee under the guise of scratching her leg. *Danielle. My parents. We'll never be found.*

The men did nothing but sit. In the shade. *La sombra.* They didn't speak to her, Wayne or Luis, and they didn't speak to each other. Somewhere, far away, a farm animal — sheep or cow — bleated. The only other sounds were the occasional buzzing of insects and the scritch of a knife on wood.

"Do you have a family, Luis?" Andrea blurted.

He had a second wife who was studying to be a teacher, three children. The oldest had *ocho años.* Eight years. A young family.

"Wow, you must be really busy," she said, her voice bouncing from word to word as if her tongue wore springs. Oh, how Canadian, she judged. What next? Start discussing the weather? But nobody discussed the weather when it was always the same, always this freaking hot. She felt as though she had something trapped in her throat — her heart, lodged up there near her tonsils. Why wasn't Wayne helping? Couldn't he think of one damned blessed thing to say?

This was the middle of it, when she was thinking about the story she would make of it one day. *Ten men and me out in the GD sticks.*

They'd been under the *palapa* for twenty-five minutes, and no buses had come or gone. She felt she needed to make some connection with the other men, reserved as they were. What they were thinking? There were seven, not the ten she'd first thought. She pulled her yard photos out and offered them to the woodcarver. The photos passed from hand to hand. Could they sense what she was feeling behind her carefree posture, her gabbing about God knew what?

The sun was at the height of its arc. Soon it would start slipping toward the sea. They might sit here all night, and she the only woman. Wayne, with his bad neck: what good would he be if it came right down to it?

"Listen, Luis, we have to get back to Puerto Vallarta soon. We're supposed to be meeting my sister and her husband." She checked her watch, hoped it wasn't too obvious. "He's a lawyer, and he might sue us if we're even one minute late. When are you going back?" A paperthin lie, but she'd managed to camouflage the desperation in her voice.

Luis told them which bus to get on, and the appropriate driver stood and started toward it. A trap? she wondered. Or could it be this easy? She shook Luis's hand again, and he bent toward her cheek. *Un besito.*

"Thanks for your help." Andrea tossed the words across her left shoulder. She wanted to bolt toward the bus, but talked her legs through their walking, feet burning in the thick socks and hiking boots, face damp and stinging as though she'd passed through a hammock of cobwebs.

They boarded the bus, dropped six pesos into the driver's cardboard collection box, and sat at the back. Wayne said nothing. And she said nothing. And they followed the same rutted road past the same shacks, the same desperate trees, the same pigs rooting in familiar ditches.

The boy and the dog were gone. Maybe she'd imagined that. She'd ask Wayne, later, when these things could be spoken of again. If either of them were to utter a solitary word now it might jinx everything.

So where were all the people? Was this bus really transporting them back to Pitillal, then on to Puerto Vallarta? Oh, she'd love to have a full-out, no holds barred, body-wracking sob session into a fist-clenched pillow right now. She took several slow, deep breaths — a skill she'd been taught in prenatal classes but promptly forgot when Danielle's head popped out enroute to the delivery room.

The bus bumped over something on the road — dog, Andrea guessed — then shuddered to a stop. A girl in a navy jumper and a white, pressed, short-sleeved shirt boarded. Her hair was neatly brushed into a ponytail; a pink plastic backpack was hooked around her wrist. School was out. She's going home, Andrea realized.

The girl sat on the opposite side, two seats ahead. She gazed at Andrea without expression for several moments. Then she smiled.

IT WAS A COSTUME PARTY WITH A 1970S THEME AND DIXON WAS making her go. "I don't like those people," Ty called from all fours inside the closet. She questioned the inherent sadism of requiring quests to assemble costumes for a party in June. Hallowe'en was bloody bad enough. New Year's freaking Eve was bad enough.

"You don't even know them," Dix quickly countered.

"Then why am I going?"

"What?" Dix shimmied a sweater over his head, messing his hair. He looked like he'd been held up by the ankles and shaken. "I can't hear you. If you want to talk come out here."

Ty backed out of the closet. She had failed to find anything suitable for the party, which was — she checked her watch — two hours away. "I said, why am I going?" Her voice was sultry, like an FM radio announcer's on a Saturday night show.

"Because they're my friends." Not entirely true, he thought; they were mostly clients, a few friends of Hugh's, employees.

"And what am I? Just your lover, your squeeze, your — "

"Sugar pie honey bunch," he sang. "You find anything?" He continued singing. Ever since Hugh had set the party theme, Dix had been inserting old rock 'n' roll lyrics into their conversations. Ty had to admit, he made his own fun.

"No, and that's the Supremes," she said, "from the '60s, not the '70s."

Dix was dressed. He'd found a pair of plaid polyester pants and a chocolate brown and navy velour sweater — the type his grandmother had given him every Christmas throughout the 1970s — at Value Village.

Strangers' clothes, Ty thought, and they smelled like strangers. He'd also bought mustard-coloured platform boots — just five bucks! — with a loose heel.

Searching for Crazy Glue knocked the next half hour off his day.

"Behind the salt and pepper shakers," Ty suggested as she riffled through a dresser drawer, "near the toothpicks."

Not there.

"By the washing machine, or maybe beside the storm windows in the garage. I think I used it out there a few months ago."

"What were you working on?" he asked.

"I don't remember. Maybe I was getting high."

This stopped him. Ty, sixteen birthdays behind him, could get a little crazy. Not psycho crazy, but oh-my-god-what-is-she-going-to-do-next crazy. Once they were test-driving a convertible with no intention of buying it — her suggestion — and she flashed two teenagers in the next lane. Well, they'd been ogling her, she said. Why not make their day? She had nice breasts, and she knew it. The kids nearly hit the ditch.

The glue was nowhere. He returned from the basement with a hammer and pounded the first of three finishing nails into the wobbly heel at an angle that he hoped wouldn't kill his feet. Ty held the boot; he hammered. "Hold it steady."

She added another hand. "I'm trying."

"Try harder."

One of the nails bent and he couldn't pull it out. It was obvious, on the public side of the heel. "Congratulations," Ty said, "it's Frankenshoe."

Dix was in a hurry to throw the costumes together and pick up booze before Ty said "Screw it!" and refused to go. Hugh was a longtime friend and his partner — in that order — at The Edge, an advertising and graphic design company with a few lucrative national accounts and a growing number of provincial government contracts. He checked himself in the dresser mirror then added the *pièce de resistance*: plastic aviator glasses with photo-grey lenses that he'd saved from high school. His left eye was much weaker than his right now; he cupped each eye, making a test. He couldn't read the numbers on the digital clock. "I'm literally half blind. Maybe I should punch the lenses out, just wear my contacts. Screw the photo-grey."

"Don't do that," Ty said, behind him. She'd found a necklace with wooden beads. "They always do that in the movies and it looks so fake."

"No, they don't do that in the movies. In the movies they use regular glass in the lenses."

"But it still looks fake."

"Yes, it still looks fake." He noticed the beads. "That's all you've got . . . a necklace?"

She held it high, like an offering.

He put his car keys in her hand, closed her fingers around them and pushed her toward the door. "Go. Find something."

"I hate these people," she said again, loudly. She didn't know why she tortured and teased him, crazy in love as she was.

Selma Pederson, next door, was watering her geraniums. She frowned at Ty. Ty meowed.

❧❧❧

"Honey, I'm home!" She poured the contents of her bag onto the dining room table. "Wa-là." Clunky, knee-high leather boots with square toes and swirls of dark brown stitching, white hoop earrings and a striped poncho. The way the earrings were looped together reminded Dix of a snowman. Ty was sporting sunglasses with round, pink lemonade-tinted lenses.

"Janis Joplin," he said, lifting one heavy boot.

"I still have to make cut-offs." She scooped her purchases. "Then I guess we can flock off."

Before they left, Dix parted Ty's hair — dyed the colour of aged plums — pulled each side into a pigtail and bound them with shoelaces; it was all he could find.

He never thought he'd become the type of guy who'd fiddle with a woman's hair, but with Ty he did these things. *Offered* to. Sometimes he washed and combed it out for her. Sometimes he let it slither through his fingers. "Leather ties would be better than these laces," he said, cheered now that Ty seemed to be getting into the spirit of things.

❧❧❧

She was driving, on account of Dix's inadequate prescription. Her beer and his Glen Livet were in the trunk. "I feel like a target in this thing," she said, plucking the poncho. "I swear if anyone I know — or anyone remotely human —

sees me like this, you're cut off for life." She often jokingly used sex as a threat, playing on the stereotypical gossip whispered behind their backs: older, financially comfortable guy; hot young trophy.

Dix and Ty knew that's what it looked like; this much was true: Dix was on his second life. In his first he'd married the sensible girl his high school teachers knew he would, had two children — now two smart-mouthed adolescents — who lived with Ann Marie in Calgary near a manmade lake with submerged lights that automatically flicked on at dusk. The children visited Dix at Easter and Thanksgiving — Ann Marie wouldn't budge on Christmas — and they had a month-long sojourn together each summer. Last summer it was a month-long ordeal. The kids hated Ty; they called her Bimbette. He was confidant they'd grow out of it. He'd remained friends with Ann Marie, which had been the problem all along. They were good buddies — and frequently mistaken for siblings — both tall and angular, with caps of dark hair, raisin-coloured eyes and noses that bordered on sharpness; attractive at a second or third glance. Intimacy felt like incest. They were good tennis partners and enjoyed beating each other at Scrabble. Ann Marie did not listen to the Tragically Hip at an ear-splitting volume — at any volume — or smoke pot or eat Kung Pao Chicken in the nude. Ty played neither tennis nor Scrabble.

They were almost there. "You're sure you don't want to quickly zip around and get the acoustic? It would really top off the costume." He'd been pushing his old guitar on her for the last twenty minutes.

"I don't play."

"So what?"

"It'd be awkward. I'd bump into everyone. I might break a lamp or poke an eye out."

"Yeah, I guess."

Judging by the number of vehicles double parked along Hugh's crescent, they were among the last to arrive. "I've just had a premonition," Ty said. "Simone's going to swing the door open, slap a manicured hand over her mouth and say, 'Oops, sorry! We forgot to tell you, we decided not to do costumes.'"

"Don't be paranoid, Darling. It doesn't become you." He rang the bell.

Simone, in a psychedelic moo-moo with orange dingle-ball earrings, led them in. "Oh, sweet!" She lifted Ty's string of beads. "Joni Mitchell!"

Next they were assaulted by a pulsing strobe. "Neat, hey?" Simone said.

"Hugh's idea. Sort of a time warp thing, to get everyone in the mood." She noticed the bottle and Ty's six pack. "You sillies . . . you didn't need to bring anything. I'll take that and be right back."

Ty whispered, "Isn't it neat! Isn't it just groovy!"

The walls were throbbing. People were dancing to Santana's "Black Magic Woman" on the hardwood, the Persian carpet — Dix knew they'd paid $8000 for it at an auction — rolled safely away. Others — Ty guessed about thirty — clustered around the room's perimeter. She dangled the sunglasses from her teeth. "What's that?" she asked out one side of her mouth and nodded toward the stereo.

"An eight track," Dix answered. "Life before CDs. Shouldn't be long before the tape gets all tangled up inside that thing — look, they've already wedged a matchbook along the side to get it to play properly. We always had to do that."

"Ah, the good old days," she said, plopping into a beanbag chair. She removed the glasses and planted them in a pot overflowing with Boston fern. The room had been stripped of anything contemporary. Swag lamps with green and orange plastic shades illuminated the corners. Two huge macramé owls stared across the dancers' heads, and a velvet Elvis painting hovered like a patriarch's portrait above the fireplace.

"You made it." Hugh slapped Dix on the shoulder and pressed Ty's middle fingers. "Like the get-up?" His flared jeans were so tight in the crotch he looked like a eunuch; black platform boots and a denim vest over an iron-on T-shirt. "I won't be able to sit down all night."

Ty stared at the iron-on: a silver-haired woman in a red swimsuit, head tipped back, forearm resting on a raised knee. More teeth than the average hyena, she thought. "Who's the chick?"

"Farrah," Hugh said.

"Fawcett," Dix added.

Ty raised her palms in the "you got me" position. She was jesting, but Hugh didn't know and Dix only suspected.

"*Charlie's Angels?* The TV show?" Hugh heard his name and looked for the source: an aide to the provincial agriculture minister. "Excuse me."

Dix flushed. Damn their age gap. Their frames of reference were completely screwed up. Ty thought the movie *Seven* was a classic, and she didn't *get* Monty Python.

Simone returned with Dix's scotch, a beer for Ty. Ty saw that the tip of the hostess's right pinky was missing. Simone smiled and fluttered away like a moth.

"Thank Christ it's their year to host the party," Dix said. He swirled the ice in his drink.

Ty was surveying the room. "If there's anything more pathetic than a bunch of . . . " she selected her next word carefully, " . . . *older* people pretending the clock stopped and doing that — " she singled out a couple hustling to "Stayin' Alive" " — I don't want to know about it."

"Be a good girl, Ty. These are my friends, this is one night." He said hello to a couple Ty didn't know. The woman, in a black catsuit, was taller than her partner.

"You didn't introduce me."

"Sorry," Dix said, "I thought you wanted to be invisible. That was Deirdre. Our accountant."

They circled the room, stopping where there was wall space near two icy blondes rapt in conversation, glasses of red wine held at bust level. Ty could taste their perfume.

"So I say to her, what are you doing, and she tells me she's solarizing. Can you believe it? Solarizing, and she's nine years old."

Simone floated up with shrimp hor d'oeuvres and whisked them beneath their noses. Dix took one.

Ty thought she could smell coffee. "I'm wondering why you never remember how I take my coffee," she said, thinking aloud. "You still don't know, do you? Because I know how you take yours. One cream, one sugar. You told me once — just once — and I never forgot."

Dix turned. Was she talking to him? She was. She had a habit of making unusual statements apropos of nothing. He had never known anyone like her. "Sorry."

"You don't have to say sorry . . . I'm not mad, just curious. And how come you can never remember my mom's name?"

"I know your mother's name. Madeline." Maybe he shouldn't have made her come, he thought, scanning the room. She truly did stick out among all the cool, coiffed women, mostly blondes, mostly statuesque (or "stacked," as his son would say), mostly wives of the ambitious men he did business with and a few of Hugh and Simone's friends tossed in. "My God . . . it's uncanny."

Ty scratched her arm. The poncho's fringes were irritating her. "What's uncanny?"

"At least a dozen women in this room could have walked straight out of a Hitchcock movie. They're Hitchcock's women — exactly the type he casted — frigid females with a vulnerable core. See that one in the orange polka dot hot pants? God, I don't remember *those* from the '70s — she's a ringer for Kim Novak in *Vertigo*. And that woman, scratching her leg? Just the way her hair's styled and the shape of her mouth . . . she could be Janet Leigh — "

"No way," Ty said, in typical deadpan.

He knew she didn't know who Janet Leigh was, or Tippi Hedren, or maybe even Grace Kelly, but she was behaving. He wondered if she felt out of her league among the rich, sophisticated gals. He would love to get inside the maze of her lovely head.

Guests were bumping into each other, stepping on each other's toes, spilling drinks, laughing, apologizing. Hugh was playing air guitar like Hendrix. The music changed again, and Dix recognized "Kung Fu Fighting." He had it on a K-Tel album. If anyone asked him to dance, he would say yes.

Ty was being dramatic with her cigarette. "Oh, I was going to tell you . . . I went through those bookshelves beneath the stairs and found your yearbooks." She flicked ashes into her bottle, which, he realized, had been empty a long time.

"Most people might look at one or two out of curiosity and put them away, but not me. I wanted to know you, like Hugh knows you, like Ann Marie does. I wanted to see if I could tell what kind of a guy you were back then, whether you were the type that went around opening doors for teachers or snapping bra straps. I found you on the basketball team . . . in a candid shot by your locker, your arm around some girl. You had those glasses on." She paused. "That's what I did for you."

"That's nice." Always this need to showcase her love, he thought, but she was also complicated, challenging — deep when you got to know her. And she liked to take the pulse of their relationship often. He hated talking about feelings, abhorred having to explain his own. And "some girl" was Ann Marie. "Ty, I've got to mingle — "

"Sure, I'll just hang."

He looked at her with his better eye. "It's safe to leave you alone?"

"Aye," she said, affecting an Irish accent, something she often did since reading *Angela's Ashes*. "I promise not to be rude to the pretty ladies. Go. Do that thing you do."

He kissed her, just below the ear. "I won't be long." She smelled like her cigarettes.

❧❧❧

It was a big house; she could meander and no one would notice. She passed three more blondes, in starchy up-dos. "Squirrels love me," the turtle-necked one was saying. "They just love me."

"Excuse me," Ty interrupted, "which way to the biff?"

"Upstairs, to the right," answered the woman whom squirrels adored.

"There's also one in the master and one downstairs."

The stairs led Ty down to a pool table, gun rack, antlers attached to the wall.

Three guys — Adidas track suit, baby blue polyester leisure suit, and black Afro wig with love beads — were playing a child's game. Adidas tracksuit noticed Ty and smiled like a birthday boy. "Battling Tops!" he enthused. "God, what a game. Remember it?"

"Like yesterday," she said.

One of his opponents began telling a joke and Ty couldn't escape. "So this woman comes home from work one day and hears buzzing from her daughter's room. She goes in and finds her daughter going at it with a vibrator. 'Sally,' she says, 'what are you doing?' and Sally says, 'Mom, I'm thirty-five, single, and I still live at home. This is as close as I'm ever going to get to a husband.' Well, her mother could see her point, so she shut the door and left her daughter alone. The next day the father comes home and hears buzzing from his daughter's room. He also finds her with Mr. Happy. 'What the hell's going on here?' he says, and Sally says, 'Dad, I'm thirty-five, single, and I still live at home. This is as close as I'm ever going to get to a husband.' What the hell, he thinks, she's likely right, and he shuts the door. A few days later Sally's mom comes home and hears the now familiar buzzing, but this time it's coming from the living room. She walks in and finds her husband sitting beside the vibrator. 'Jesus H Christ, Bill, what are you doing?' she asks, and he says, 'Watching the ball game with my son-in-law.'"

Ty found the bathroom. She opened the shower doors and discovered dirty sweatsocks. Hugh's son's, she thought. The one in college. Dix liked him.

She slipped past the game players and up the carpeted stairs, feeling the weight of her boots. A black Lab bolted around a corner and sniffed her thighs. "Finally," she said, rubbing his nose, "someone I can talk to." The dog allowed her to scratch his back until the doorbell rang and he howled away.

Up another flight, Ty spied a couple at either end of a futon. "Listen, I think we know each other pretty well now," the woman was saying, "and I think I can cut to the chase. Are you attracted to me?"

Ty backed out and bumped into Dix. "Hey, do I know you?" he asked.

"I don't know. Are you rich?"

"Loaded."

"Married?"

"Not recently."

She laced her fingers into his.

"Listen, a bunch of us are playing a game downstairs. I told them I was going to be right back. I thought maybe you'd left."

Ty raised her eyebrows. "Really?"

"Yeah, I haven't seen you, so — "

"Would you have been upset?"

"God . . . yes! These are my friends, you're the woman I love. You're unpredictable. I want everyone to be happy. I want everyone to be friends."

"Spoken like a true drunk," she said, "but come on, admit it, you love that I'm unpredictable."

She's so smart, he thought. Everyone should know this secret.

"What's the game?"

"Dividing the world."

"That's the name of the game?"

"That's it. Everyone says how they divide the world. You know, Coke drinkers vs. Pepsi. People that wave when you pull over to let them pass and those assholes who don't. How do you divide the world?"

She thought about it and smirked. "Between those who liked *Pulp Fiction* and those idiots who didn't."

"Perfect," he said, smiling, because he knew she knew that he'd walked out of it and she'd raved about Tarentino's film. "Let's go."

In the basement, three men, including Adidas track suit, and five women were relaxing on the floor. "Maybe I'll just watch," Ty said, dropping Dix's hand. She sat on the empty couch.

"Oh, come on," Dix said quietly, "play."

She shook her head.

Dix sat between one of Hitchcock's women — in red, white and blue striped pants with a matching fringed vest — and Deirdre. "I'm back."

A man in a toga said, "I divide the world between those who like cats and those who prefer dogs."

"Yeah," Dix agreed. "Good one. Dogs rule! Pineapple on pizza or not."

Track suit stretched his long legs. "Those who believe in UFOs and those who don't. Personally, I'm convinced they exist."

One of the frosty blondes blurted, "Shoppers or not . . . black licorice or red."

Before long ideas were being fired out like random missiles: "Sinkers or swimmers! Domestic or foreign! Cars, that is. Boxers or briefs! Watch wearers or not! Sunworshippers versus sun blockers! IBMs or Macs! Handy or helpless! Baths or showers! Nude or pyjamas! Those who would bungy jump, those who would not, not for a million bucks."

Dix made eye contact with Ty, then got caught up in the game again.

"I've got one," Deirdre said. "Circumcised or not."

"That's how you divide the world?" Toga asked.

"Well . . . " Deirdre buried her face.

The dog ran into the room ahead of two newcomers.

"Hey, Jason!" Dix said, a little too loudly. Everyone turned. Hugh's son and a friend were creeping downstairs. Ty guessed they would have preferred to go unnoticed. A woman whose eyes seemed to be peering in opposite directions swung her arms around Jason. He looked terrified. He quickly shook her off and disappeared into his room.

The friend was less intimidated. He stood behind the game players, hands stuffed in the front pockets of his baggy jeans. He was older than Jason, Ty thought — maybe twenty-five: her age — tall but proportionately muscled, dark hair stylishly messed, a gold hoop in one eyebrow. He caught her gaze and casually approached. She gave him a half-smile.

"So how do you divide the world?" he asked, softly. No one else heard.

She laughed. "Between people who get off on games like this and those of us who don't."

"I hear that." He sat beside her, their knees close together. "I'm Aidan."

"Ty. Do you go to school with Jason?"

"No, I don't live here. Jason's mom and my mom are sisters."

"That would make you cousins."

"Good one."

She was perspiring in her poncho but didn't want to take it off. She'd been a little too aggressive with the scissors and had cut the shorts too short, even for short shorts. "So where's home, Aidan?"

"Halifax."

"You kid me! I was in Halifax two years ago. While I was there Arnold Schwarzenegger and his family docked their yacht. I didn't see him, but it was in the papers." She saw that Aidan had green, dreamy eyes and wasn't afraid to look directly into hers. Young men, she thought. So bold. "You been here before?"

"Just once, when I was about five."

"So how do you like it? Having a good time?"

"Yeah, it's good," he said, holding her gaze. "Right at this moment I'm loving it."

❧❧❧

Shadows at the back of the large hexagonal yard.

Aidan passed the joint and she took another toke. Fractions of conversations reached their small party in the dewy grass. "Fearful of everything," someone said. "Only on Sundays." Occasionally a single word floated back. "Amsterdam." "Bastard." It was all hilarious; she loved the way Aidan laughed.

Ty rested her back against the six-foot cedar fence. She had pulled her poncho as far back as possible so there was a small triangle to sit on. It was tight against her neck, like a choker. "This is good shit," she said, returning the joint.

"Yeah, good Maritime shit." He inhaled, letting his forearm rest on her knee. She took the final toke, flicked what was left into the grass before it burnt her tweezed fingers: no roach clip.

Aidan moved so that they were facing each other, knee to knee. He put one hand on the back of her neck. He didn't kiss her, just moved in as if he was going to. She touched his cheek and dragged her fingers across his lips. He caught her fingertips in his mouth and gently sucked them. This was all slow. Then his hand was beneath her poncho, inside her bra, cupping her breast. He still hadn't kissed her. He circled her nipple with his thumb.

She grabbed his wrist. "Sorry, I can't."

"You're with one of those guys in there?"

"I'm with one of those guys."

He slid his hand out, ran it through his hair. "Why?"

She hardly paused at all. "I love one of those guys."

"Okay," he said, standing and brushing grass off his pants. "That's cool."

"No offense, that was nice, that *would* have been nice, but — "

"Really," he said, hands back at home in his pockets, "it's okay. I respect that."

દ∾∾∾

"We could take a taxi," Dix was saying, head like a cannonball against the backrest. He'd pay for those last three shooters in the morning. "We probably should."

"I've only had a few drinks," Ty said, signaling to merge onto the freeway. "Close your eyes . . . when you open them we'll be home."

He was happy to comply, but soon she was speaking again. "What do you love about us? Not about me, but about us."

Lord. He was too tired for talk. Too wasted. "I love that there *is* an us. That you put up with me."

"You didn't put any thought into that," she said. "But that's okay. You know what I love? I love that we invite stares and speculation. I love that we can have a perfectly good time staying home on a Saturday night. I love that you don't even know how totally unhip you are sometimes. It's . . . refreshing."

"I try."

They were quiet then. Dix slipped into sleep. The city appeared to be sleeping, too, Ty thought. She loved the view from the top of the University Bridge, the way downtown lights reflected in the river and the Bessborough Hotel castled against the shore. I should come out here with a camera, capture this, she thought, but realized how difficult that might be, like her attempts with lightning and the moon.

"We're home," she said, gently shaking Dix's arm.

Inside she flung off the poncho, kicked out of the heavy boots, winged shorts, panties, camisole and bra as she passed from room to room. She flopped naked onto the bed, and moaned.

Dix burrowed in beside her. "Your feet are cold." He took them between his own.

"I'm beat," she said. "I've hit the wall."

"I'm drunk. I've hit the wall, too."

Her body was leaving the waking world in stages: fingertips, hands, arms, shoulders, head. She was thinking about the scar that slashed Dix's right knee in half, a surgery of some sort, years before she'd met him. She wanted that story, too. She needed everything, everything. To be so filled with all his details the scars between them blurred.

BABY PLEASE DON'T GO

IT WAS HOTTER THAN HADES THE SUMMER OF 1982 AND I HAD A perpetual headache. I wasn't used to that much sun. We were smack dab in the heart of Medicine Hat, where you'd trip over a rattlesnake if you weren't watching. Each morning I'd wake up in our cheap one-bedroom to find the mercury already climbing — you could smell it happening, a stink like scorched cotton those days Mama forgot herself with the iron — then I'd roll off the damp sheets, finger-rake my long hair and wonder how the hell I'd got there and who'd made off with my real life.

Burn had a low-paying job repairing TVs and stereos that kept me free of him for nine-hour stretches. He left early with his brown bag lunch. The three things he ever told me about his line of work I remember to this day: AM stands for amplitude modification, FM means frequency modulation, and LED is short for light emitting diode. Three tiny bites of info that I've never dropped into a conversation in my life, three more clots of knowledge that take up space in my brain but never do me a damn bit of good.

I was twenty-one, and slowly dying.

He'd brought me there in the night. I must have been wiped from the long drive up from Three Forks, Montana, and dazed by the city lights, which made me think of Las

Vegas. The road curved up and around steep hills; the streets of San Francisco to my small-town eyes. I kept forgetting we were in Canada now. Burn was a Canuck, born and duly raised. My birth certificate read Canada, too, but my folks fell into the one-time luck of inheriting an American uncle's land; they'd hopscotched the border before I was old enough to tie my shoes.

Burn brought me back on the premise of fun times, decent sex and easy employment, and my bald thirst for adventure kicked into gear like some kind of fancy sportscar built for two. All mag wheels, and dual exhaust. There were other things, too. He wasn't a mean drunk, he knew a bit about motors and constellations, and I got off on the way I'd ask him something and he'd just let the question hang there for a few moments, suspended between us like clouds in a comic book conversation. He wasn't much of a talker from the get-go — my ex'd been in love with the drama of his own voice — and when he did answer he spoke real slow, as if waiting for exactly the right size and shape of words to rise up inside him before he opened his trap.

We bunked with his parents that first night, slept in separate rooms. After we turned in I crossed my arms behind my head and stared at the model airplanes dangling from his bedroom ceiling. Every once in a while one of them would take a quarter spin and it was there, sandwiched between his cowboy sheets, my feet pinned back at unnatural angles, that the first worm of doubt crawled through my veins.

The next morning I helped his father with breakfast dishes. Burn's dad was what polite folks call a heavy-set man; a retired school principal with his office nameplate nailed to the family's front door. He wore slip-on shoes so he wouldn't have to bend, the backs of his plaid slippers permanently crushed for immediate access. While Burn and his mom yacked in the living room and the Shih Tzu worked herself into a licking frenzy on her toes, I washed and Burn's pop dried. He asked me to rewash one fork and two glasses. We found our own apartment that afternoon.

In the early days I explored the city on foot, but there wasn't much of anything to discover beyond an exceptional thrift shop where I bought a sweater the colour of algae for one quarter. I wore it over my tanktop, then limped up the long hill home, sweat pooling beneath my breasts. The second and third times I made the journey, a couple of British soldiers from the Suffield base stopped me for cigarettes. I could hardly afford my own habit; I'd be damned if I was going to support anyone else's.

At first I couldn't buy a job, despite my dual citizenship. I had nine months of secretarial school behind me and thought the world would be clamouring after my sixty-five-words-per-minute and Forkner shorthand, but everyone was talking recession and nobody had openings, nobody was bloody likely to.

"But don't give up," Burn would say, coming home after a day in the shop to find me with my hand in a bag of peanuts or sucking the chocolate skin off an After Eight, the TV tuned to "Another World." He'd go shower then, and when he came back we'd pull the blinds and start out on the couch, staying there to do the wild thing if we passed a certain point and couldn't make it to the bed. That, at least, was working well for us. After, Burn would hold me against him, wrapping his brown arms and white legs around me like a cage, and he'd make me promise I'd never leave.

"Cross my heart," I'd say, mumbling it into his neck or chest, whichever part of him I was jammed against. He was five years older and had been engaged once. It was the girl that checked out, not him. He was the one that got burned.

I followed a lead in the paper and got myself hired as a Hostess hostess. My job was to stand in the middle of a Hostess potato chip display at the local Kmart and offer samples to the passersby. If I could sell them a bag, all the better. Most folks took the samples and didn't buy, but lots flat out ignored me.

Fact is, I wasn't much to look at that summer. The hot air and dust had conspired against my hair, and with the vacant days spent snacking in front of the television, then having all those chips in my face, I was inviting pounds like they were the latest rage, mostly on my hips and bust. The extra fifteen made me even hotter. My skin was a nylon suit two sizes too small. Itchy. "Fuck it," I said, pinching three floppy inches of flesh below my ribs before I wiggled into the red Hostess skirt. "Fuckshitdamn."

Burn started to change around the end of July. Instead of wanting sex after his showers, he'd prop pillows against the headboard of our second-hand bed, pick up his red Fender Stratocaster, plug in the amp and say, "Call me when supper's ready." Then I'd hear him pluck out a blues riff, the same thing over and over again, thirty times or more. If it wasn't that, it was a tape: the Amboy Dukes with Ted Nugent on guitar, smouldering through "Baby Please Don't Go" at a volume I was sure Burn's parents could hear on the other side of the Hat.

I didn't know what was happening, didn't know if it was the oppressive heat, his kiss-ass job, me, or those Sunday dinners with his folks where they'd make us play mah-jongg and drink herbal tea until we felt drunk, and I'd have to kick Burn under the kitchen table to make him take us home. I was kind of floating there myself, waiting for the right moment to bolt.

We were six weeks into our cohabitation when I saw the sign taped to the wall in the coin-op laundry room. Wanted, it said, someone in the building to babysit three-year-old boy, weekday afternoons and evenings. A phone number was printed on the fringes scissored into the bottom of the page, but no one had pulled any off. The Hostess job was only three mornings a week and if I was going to split I'd need cash; I threw Burn's work pants into the washer, pulled off a tab and dragged myself back upstairs to call.

The woman at the end of the phone was Carmen, from the top floor. I didn't know her, wasn't sure I'd ever seen her, as she came and went through the north end of the building and Burn and I used the south. "Come on up," she said, "I'll put the coffee on." She sounded like a nice person.

I left a note for Burn because it was Saturday and he was helping his brother move into a duplex. Burn was pretty used to finding me at home by now, so I thought I'd better leave notice. I still carried a fraction of hope for us, but it was basically a losing proposition, like trying to light a cigarette in the wind.

The hallway on the third floor smelled like East Indian spices and an oil change, neither of which mixed well with the heat. I knocked on 313, the last number at the end of the hall, and thanked Jesus that we were on the main. "Hello," Carmen said, opening the door in bare feet, frayed cut-offs and a halter top that drew attention to her flat breasts. I stepped past a thin tabby on its way out. Another cat, an orange shorthair with one and a half ears, curled around the kitchen corner. The smell of cat — cat piss, cat food, cat shit — was almost audible. I stifled a cough. Then Carmen's boy came scooting up on a red tractor he pushed with his feet — something he'd already outgrown — and stopped inches from my toes. "This is Jojo. Jojo, this is Thea, the lady who's going to be taking care of you."

"Hi Jojo." I stuck out my hand. He just looked at it, so I ruffled his hair instead. I didn't remember accepting the job, but after a strong cup of coffee and half a dry doughnut I found myself doublechecking that she needed me at 3:00 on Monday, not 3:30. Carmen worked at the Sands till 11:00, and she'd always, always be home before midnight. I could open a can of this or that — spaghetti or ravioli — for Jojo's supper. "He doesn't eat much," she said. "Eats like a friggin' bird."

❧❧❧

Burn thought it was a good move. "I wasn't going to say nothing but I don't like you working over there in the mall, 'specially in that little ass-hugging skirt. How's a girl supposed to have any self-respect in something like that?"

Yeah, Burn, I felt like saying. Like you know about self-respect; college grad working for fifty cents above minimum wage. It'd be five years before he could see his way over the mountain of student loan debt.

Sunday passed with the same uneventfulness I was getting used to. We slept late, did the last few days' worth of dishes, complained that there was nothing but shit on TV. It surprised me that Burn could grow up in a place and have so few friends.

"It's a principal's kid thing," he said when I finally grew the balls to ask. He was tuning his guitar. The B string was especially sensitive.

"Yeah, but you've been out of school for what . . . seven, eight years?"

He hesitated, as always, before he spoke. "The Hat ain't that big." He plucked the temperamental B string again. "People don't forget."

Monday came and I didn't know what to do with the hours between lunch and 3:00, but sitting there at the table examining the fine red lines in my knuckles seemed like a powerful waste of time, so I got up and went into our bedroom. I poked around Burn's sheet music and guitar magazines, but I couldn't read music and only got a quarter of the way through an article on "the legendary" Buddy Guy. Suddenly my half of the dresser seemed to be calling, so I set out to organize.

I'd never been a folder — stuff and mix was more my style — but after removing the pants and shirts I'd grown too big for, I folded the remaining clothes and separated them into piles: underwear, T-shirts, shorts, and other, which included bathing suits, three pairs of knee-high hose, a tensor bandage and a black negligee that felt like oil in my fingers — an item borrowed from my oldest sister back in the day. Then I wandered into the bathroom, crawled onto the counter and started snipping the dry ends off my hair.

At 2:55 I pounded up the two flights to Carmen's, wheezing only a little. I didn't have to knock; the door was open and she had one red, stiletto-heeled foot already pointing toward the hall. She pushed her hair back and up. There were pounds of it — dyed the colour of Kansas corn since I'd last seen her — with a few loose ringlets dangling in front of her ears like sprung mattress springs. "There's Cokes in the fridge. Bedtime at 8:00." She slipped a cigarette between cherry-glossed lips and dug in her handbag, for a light, I suppose. "Oh, I just about forgot." She pressed a scrap of paper into my hand with a number scribbled on it, her long nails barely scraping my palm, like a tickle. "Call me if you have any trouble."

Jojo was on his tractor, staring up through bangs that looked like they'd been sawed off, rather than cut. I closed the door and bent, my knees cracking in unison. I pushed his bangs aside to see his eyes, clearly, for the first time. What I saw there nearly split my heart in two. "So, looks like it's you and me, kiddo." A kitten the colour of tires lept onto my lap. "Whoa, hey, where'd you come from? How many kitties do you have, Jojo?"

The boy held up four fingers. "Tree."

❧❧❧

It would be fair to say that it was an easy job. I pretty much did what I'd been doing downstairs — watching TV, snacking — except now I'd take breaks in my routine to slide a wooden puzzle together or read a Dr. Seuss. Jojo liked me. He'd snuggle up against me and we'd watch the soaps together, or he'd grab my hand when I decided I'd had enough of the cats' stench, and we'd walk to a school playground, two blocks away.

I liked him, too. He was a cool kid, the kind strangers smiled at. A little withdrawn perhaps, but I'd sit him on the swings, tell him to hang on tight and give him underducks until he squealed. I enjoyed hearing him laugh — the sound soap bubbles would make if they could — so I played the clown with him, wearing plastic mixing bowls on my head or putting on a puppet show, my hands dancing inside socks. One afternoon at the playground, a mother joined me on the park bench while Jojo and her two boys made trails in the sandbox and pushed imaginary cars. "He looks so much like you," she said, and I felt a surge of pure, sweet joy.

Sometimes Burn would come up after work. "Cute little ankle biter," he said once, throwing a foam ball for Jojo to chase like you'd throw a stick for a dog, "but what's up with his eyes?"

"What do you mean?" I looked at Jojo and saw the warm, wiry body that I snatched up several times a day and held close to my heart while Eskimo-rubbing my nose against his head. I took a phantom breath of Johnson's Baby Shampoo: the scent of his fine hair.

Burn cracked the beer he'd brought up with him. "He's a little blue beneath the eyes, don't you think? And skinny for a kid, like an Ethiopian the way his belly sticks out."

"Jojo," I called, "come here, Sweetie."

The boy ran back with the ball and stood in front of the TV: knob-kneed legs, saggy training pants, T-shirt with a huge grape popsicle stain front and centre. I planted a kiss on my palm and touched it to his cheek. "That's it, you can play now."

"Play with me?"

"Sure, why don't you get your blocks?" I watched him tear down the hall toward his room, where toys were scattered across the carpet and at least one cat would be curled on the nest of clothes in the corner.

I started bringing apples, oranges and raisins from home. I chopped up carrots and stuffed them into little bags, and I'd sneak up a can of peas or corn from the cupboard after Burn bought groceries, hoping he wouldn't notice.

ৼৼৼ

I didn't meet the boyfriend until week three. "Thea, this is Hal . . . Hal, Thea." He'd come home with Carmen after work on a Thursday, a lumbering, thick-armed man with a three-day beard and no ass. He filled the apartment doorway. It was five to twelve. Carmen's returns had been creeping closer to the midnight hour.

"Hi," I said, waiting for him to decide whether we'd shake hands or not. We didn't.

"Hey," he said. It was more of a belch than a word.

I told Carmen that I thought Jojo was coming down with a summer cold. "He's got the sniffles," I said, "and he just doesn't have his usual amount of get up and go. Could be the ca — "

"Thanks for letting me know," Carmen was saying. I wasn't focusing on her. I was looking over her shoulder at Hal's shit kickin' boots, propped on the pillows at the end of the couch where Jojo often laid his head.

The only activity he'd been interested in for the past several days was pushing the magnetic alphabet letters around on the fridge. I'd been trying to teach him things, simple things. C-A-T. "Cat, just like that. Now you try," but he seemed most impressed by the colours. He lined the magnets up in combinations that pleased him, rather than by the sounds I told him they made. Earlier that day I'd picked up the "J", a watery purple. "'J', the first letter of your name, Jojo, and this — " I slid a canary yellow "O" across the fridge, "this is an 'O'. 'J-O'. That makes the first part of your name, and the second part — " I searched the front of the fridge, then the side that wasn't crammed up next to the cupboard for another "J", but couldn't find one, so I used the same letter over again, hopping it over the "O" like a checkers piece, "the second part is the same as the first. 'J-O'. Pretty neat, hey? You've got a pretty neat name."

৵৵৵

On Friday Burn phoned when Jojo was having his nap. He felt like going out.

"Can't. Got to babysit. You go ahead though, if you want."

"Is something wrong? You're . . . I don't know, you seem to be pulling away from me."

I could have thrown our curious lack of sex in his face, but I wasn't up for a fight. Plus, I was missing a major moment in the soap: a plane was going down in the Amazon jungle while a woman about to deliver twins was screaming blue murder at her lover, the pilot, who was suffering a heart attack in the cockpit.

"Nothing, nothing's going on. I'm just beat after I'm done here. It's hard work looking after a kid all day, you know. You've got to play, all the time."

Silence. "You're planning something. You're going to leave."

"Hello? Anybody out there? I just finished saying there's nothing going on. Go out. Have a blast. I hear there's strippers at one of the hotel bars."

"Promise you're not leaving?"

"I solemnly do declare," I said, annoyed at his persistence, this weak side of himself he was displaying. I like a guy who keeps his tears and neuroses to himself.

He didn't go out. He came upstairs and played crib with me until Carmen and Hal came in with whisky so thick on their tongues and breath I had to step back. It was 12:30.

Back in our own apartment, I hit the sheets. "Aren't you coming?" I called. I'd left Burn on the couch, where he was playing his Fender without the amp plugged in. I could hear the streaking sound of his fingers on the strings, like someone wiping a window clean. I was used to sleeping beside him. I'd grown to need his rhythmic breathing in my ear before I could fall asleep. "Burn?"

"In a minute," he said.

I tried lying on my side, my stomach. The extra weight had shifted to my gut and I played with the wobbly flesh there, pinching it, wishing I could slice it off. I imagined taking a steak knife and performing the surgery myself — scraping away the blubber, then stitching up the incision with Burn's fishing line. "Burn! When you coming?"

He didn't answer. Then I heard Ted Nugent's jumpy, definitive intro on the stereo and I knew I'd lost Burn for the night.

જીજીજી

A week to the day, I found myself in a piss-poor mood. The heat hadn't let up one iota, even though we were waist deep into August. The headaches weren't unbearable but they were always there, bull's eye, right above my nose. Burn was downstairs watching TV, where he could listen at whatever volume he wanted to. I liked to keep it low after eight, so Jojo could get a good night's sleep.

At ten I made myself a cup of tea. I could smell cat stronger than ever, so I knew I must have forgotten to close the door to the storage room, where the pack of them shared one litter box. I couldn't even look at the thing — for fear it might be writhing — let alone hold my breath long enough to clean it. I closed the door, then peeked in on Jojo. He was on his back, bangs partly hiding his sleeping eyes. I opened his window as far as I could and breathed in the night, then pulled a sheet over top of him, standing there for a moment, my hand on the small bones of his chest, feeling his warmth slide right up my arm.

Carmen's door was open. I'd avoided her room, except when Jojo asked me to dig something out from under the bed — a ball or his watergun — but I was bored, and pissed that it was already 12:48 and she hadn't called, hadn't apologized or offered more money for all the times she'd been late. I walked in, surveying the unmade bed, high-heels pitched by the closet, lipsticks, blush and tubes of mascara littered across the dresser along with big, hooped earrings and used cotton balls, Jojo's stuffed panda. I opened her closet and fanned my hands against the shoulders of her outfits, making the hangers ting against each other. She had a lot of clothes, mostly clingy dresses and dark blouses; not the kinds of things I would ever wear.

I moved to the dresser and set my cup down. *Baby please don't go.* I thought I could hear Burn's music riding up the two flights of stairs and down the hallway, but in another second it was gone and the only sound was the tabby scratching its nails along the carpet, then me sliding out Carmen's top dresser drawer.

Push-up bras, red panties, a silk scarf. My eyes got stuck on the other items: a flesh-toned vibrator, handcuffs, something with balls and wires that looked foreign and torturous. I slammed the drawer, wiped my hands on my shirt, watched myself back out of the room between Jojo-sized smudges in the full-length mirror.

෧෧෧

On Saturday it started to spit rusty slivers of rain, as though God Himself was chewing snuff up there in the heavens.

Precipitation of any colour was rare as luck, so when it came I took it as a sign. "My head's splitting, Burn. We're out of everything. Could you get me some Aspirin at the drugstore? Oh, and your brother called when you were in the shower. Said he wanted you to go over there — something about a friend of his, some guy looking to buy a guitar. A bass, I think."

"Which friend?"

"I don't remember, Ron or Rob or something. He said to go over."

The lie worked as well as a sharp knife on day-old bread. While Burn was gone I scooped the contents of my side of the dresser into a suitcase, dumped my cosmetics and birth control pills into a bag, grabbed the framed photo of myself off the TV and whipped up my shoes in the hall closet. I left my red Hostess skirt on the bed, right where my hips would be I if I was lying there next to Burn. I knew when the bus was leaving. I had to work fast.

I probably didn't need to do it that way. It smacked of a getaway, and, in a sense, I suppose it was. I was a few minutes early to board, so I flipped through a *National Enquirer*, an uneasy feeling choking its way up my throat. I kept glancing over my shoulder, expecting to see Burn tearing into the place and shooting the works of us down — well, me and the old lady knitting booties on the opposite bench, which was the works of us. Everyone knows it's the quiet ones you can't trust.

I had enough money to get back to my parents' place, then I'd push off again, maybe south this time, maybe see what all the fuss about L.A. was for.

Soon enough I'd have to quit running around and make a real, grown-up life, but not yet.

I thought about how Burn used to take my feet in his lap, and the good hard rubs he gave. It hadn't been bad, there, with Burn; I'd seen sorrier times. For some girls it may have been enough, but as the bus backed out of the station and the highway rolled out before me like undeveloped film, I knew I'd never be sorry for what I'd left him with: three dirty ashtrays, two damp towels and four rooms emptied of what he presumed was love.

SOMEWHERE IN SOUTH AMERICA

REIMER IS SOMEWHERE IN SOUTH AMERICA, A PLACE HE, ANDIE and Rebecca often travel to in his dreams. It's truly a gift to fall asleep and find himself at the opposite end of the world against a backdrop of palms. There they own a beachhouse with tile floors. In the late mornings, before the humidity peaks, their bare feet slap down a sandy road to the neighbouring village. They barter in Spanish with smiling locals, buy *queso*, *leche*, *huevos*. At night, while they dream sleep, the ocean swells and churns outside their windows. The violent surf crashes inches from their door. Will the beachhouse be smashed, his family swept out to sea? The dream's so real he's convinced they could be, but the possibility doesn't jar him from his cocoon of sleep.

Always in the morning, the dream morning, they wake to exotic bird song and an ocean still as ice. Reimer's skin glistens with salt and sweat. Then he and his girls wander onto the ribbed sand to collect shells and other marine matter the ocean has left as gifts. They swim in the crystalline water, or build creatures and castles in the sand before their daily sojourn to the market.

In reality he's never left the prairie. He's never seen the ocean on either side of Canada, but this particular dream has become so familiar it feels, most of all, like home.

Andie swings a leg across him; the true morning materializes through a jungle mist.

"It's seven o'clock and time for the news," an announcer chirps. Reimer squints at the clock radio's glowing red numerals. Already? Christ.

"Morning," Andie mumbles, her mouth pressed into her pillow.

"Yes it is," he says. He touches her cheek and she opens one eye.

The door opens and Rebecca patters across the carpet in pyjamas with feet. Reimer swings her into bed between them. "Good sleep, Princess?"

"Uh uh." She fist-rubs her eyes. "I had a night dream."

Again. "Shhh . . . " Andie smooths their daughter's white-blonde hair. "Just a dream, Honey."

Reimer knows Andie's repose is forced; these five simple words undo her, and he's not thrilled about them either. When he was a kid it was vampires and being buried alive. Nightmares seem to go with the territory of childhood, he thinks. Andie says even ordinary objects can trigger a young imagination. The circus clown in the picture above her childhood bed floated away from its frame and stalked her from every corner of the room. Lamp shades distorted into faces. We each entertained a shape for what lurked beneath the bed, she reasoned. Many of us still do.

"Do you want to tell us about it?" Andie asks.

"I forget," Rebecca says. She squirms out of the valley between their bodies. "Let's get up."

Moments later they hear her preparing a bowl of cereal in the kitchen. She's more mature and independent than other five-year-olds, he thinks. Well-adjusted. Everyone says so.

"Another 'night dream'?" Andie tugs the covers and pushes Reimer toward the cliff — Rebecca's word — of the bed. "You know she doesn't forget."

"She might." He opens the blinds to a view of other grey highrise apartment buildings like their own, and wonders, again, how the city got so damn ugly.

"Come on, Reimer. Six nightmares in four weeks and you don't think she remembers?"

He watches Andie slip out of her satin nightshirt and pad naked across the room. She has broad shoulders, like a swimmer; a woman comfortable in her skin. They met when he signed up for a drawing workshop at the university: she was the model. Twenty minutes per pose for two hours of sketching. He fell for the long line of her back, the bones of her feet. Later she laughed about the thin young student with charcoal on his fingers who refused to meet her eyes.

He examines his pupils in the dresser mirror for a sign of where his own dreams have taken him. Andie appears in the reflection: handfuls of thick brown hair tousled from sleep, cheeks flushed as though they have just made love.

"But why would she lie?" Reimer asks.

Andie crosses and rubs her arms. "Maybe it's too terrifying to tell."

❧❧❧

Reimer accelerates up the incline of the underground parkade. It's a half hour drive to work, but he doesn't mind. It gives him time to think about how he's become a thirty-one-year-old man in a silver sedan on a busy freeway, appearing to all the world like he knows exactly where he's going. His life's work is in planning, in blueprints and details, but the blueprints he designed for his own life are lost.

Andie became pregnant while they were still in university. They had wanted a family, but hadn't expected one so soon. "An act of God," she called it. At the end of the school year they had a quiet wedding in his parents' back yard while neighbours watched from their windows. Andie took a three-year hiatus from her studies after Rebecca was born and only recently completed her degree in occupational therapy. When Andie returned to school, her mother stepped in to babysit, and now she watches Rebecca while Andie applies and interviews for scarce positions. Doris and Rebecca are very close. Tight, he thinks. That's what kids these days would say. They are tight.

He idles at an intersection. An ambulance speeds past; the hospital where Rebecca was born — a long, difficult labour and delivery, though Andie refused an epidural and never cried out — is two blocks west. He remembers holding his newborn daughter — the weight of a bag of potatoes — and wondering at the speed of life. The baby slept almost immediately after birth, but later, when she woke in her bassinet beside Andie's bed, her cry rattled them all. He couldn't move, couldn't do anything to soothe that red, wailing bundle he'd help create. What kind of father was he? Doris appeared with a spray of yellow roses. She lifted Rebecca from her plastic cage and left the room with her. At the end of the hall, grandmother and granddaughter were a rocking silhouette framed in a glass-bricked window and the sun's white light.

He pulls into his parking stall and stares at the sleek building where his name is on a door, nine floors up. He's found his way once again. What luck.

❧❧❧

The week unravels into Friday night and Reimer wants nothing more than to stretch out on the couch and stay there, possibly forever. The construction of the new recreational facility has been proceeding as scheduled and only slightly over budget. As the youngest architect in the department he feels his every move is under glass. There's no margin for mistakes, not now, when he and Andie are struggling to put their financial lives into something that resembles order.

"Any mail?" he asks, setting his briefcase out of sight and mind behind the closet door.

"No news is good news," she says, but he can sense her disappointment and knows better than to attempt to placate her when she's in a blue mood. She has an appetite for occasional light depression, even enjoys it, he thinks, in the same way a person delights in rubbing sore muscles.

"We're not doing anything tonight . . . why don't you and your mom go out? Beck and I can watch *The Lion King*."

"Again?" Andie manages a smile. The day's make-up has worn thin and he notes a light spray of freckles has made its annual summer appearance beneath her eyes.

He loosens his tie, a bold red one with Disney cartoon characters on it that he'd been embarrassed to wear to work, even though his partners wear similar ties, as if to suggest that there's more to them than dark suits, pressed shirts and corporate hair. "Why not?" He fumbles with his shirt buttons and Andie's fingers move in.

"You don't mind?"

"Trust me, I'm whipped."

She gives his chin a squeeze. "I'll see if Mom's free."

❧❧❧

He doesn't expect her back early. He clears dinner dishes, then runs a tub for Rebecca. After her bath she fetches popcorn from the cupboard and holds the bag out to him. "Make lots, Daddy."

He pours a few kernels into the pot. "Is that enough?"

"No!" She giggles at the routine.

He adds a few more kernels. "Is that enough?"

"No!" She watches him pour again, the kernels falling in a beaded stream.

"How about that? Enough now?"

She shakes her head.

"Okay, just a little bit more."

He pops enough to fill a wok, then they settle on the couch to watch the video. Soon Rebecca sleeps. He carries her to her room, which is not pink and fussy like his nieces' rooms, but splashed with colour and bold designs. "Goodnight, Princess." He tucks her in, thanks the God of his youth for the blessing of such a normal, happy — everyone says so — child.

An aquarium gurgles across the room. Reimer sprinkles several fish flakes onto the rippling water and Jazzy, Cinnamon and Big Boy — the goldfish Rebecca's named as if they're kittens — leave the lacy plants to dart to the surface.

Back on the couch, South America comes quickly.

They are snorkelling near a coral reef. The colours are so vivid he can almost taste them: the peppermint green of Andie's swimsuit; the school of icicle blue pencil fish, inches from his mask; the watermelon-coloured coral beneath his daughter's inquisitive hands.

"Daddy!"

"I'm right here," he says, but his voice is garbled by the snorkel and salt water burns his throat.

"Daddy! Wake up!"

Moments pass before he realizes that this child, socking him hard with her small fists, is his real-world daughter.

"Daddy — night dream!"

He gropes for the lamp. "It's okay, I'm here . . . Daddy's here."

She is white as bleached bone. He pulls her on top of him and holds her tightly, rubbing circles on her back. "Shhh, shhh. It was just a dream. Just a bad, bad dream."

She sobs and convulses in his arms. "It's all over the floor . . . I stepped in it!"

Stepped in it? "What? What is it?" He desperately wants to slap his hands over his ears.

"Water!"

The time on the VCR flashes 11:30. He needs Andie to be home.

જ જ જ

He knows the smell. A warm smell reminiscent of childhood, morning, his mother offering porridge with a crown of brown sugar. Andie veers toward him, a breakfast tray balanced in her hands. She sets it across his lap and lifts the covering bowl. A gecko skitters off the plate.

"Wha . . . ?"

"Hey! Where were you?" she asks.

"Andie?"

"You were expecting someone else?" She sets the toast and coffee on the bedside table. "Some night, huh?"

"Yeah, some night." He leans over to grasp the mug. Ceramic. Real. A wedding gift from one of his college

92

roommates who opted out of figure drawing because he couldn't do hands or faces. Andie ruffles his hair like he's a boy or a puppy. He sips the coffee.

"She didn't say anything else?"

"That's it."

"It must be the aquarium. That gurgling all the time . . . those bug-eyed fish. They'd give me the creeps too."

"I'll empty it today."

She sighs, like it's something she's been holding in a long time. "And the fish?"

"I'll take care of them."

Andie sits on the bed and smooths the sheet. "Mom's concerned."

"Your mother knows?"

"She thinks Beck should stay with her this weekend, see if it makes a difference."

Reimer swallows more of the strong instant coffee. He doesn't touch the toast, couldn't eat if he wanted to. "What do you think?"

"It's definitely worth a try."

ชชช

They pack Rebecca's clothes and her favourite toys — a stuffed polar bear, an exotic doll that sings when squeezed, crayons and colouring books—and drive across the city. Doris lives in a small, wartime house in an aging neighbourhood where the residents keep the grass green, hedges trimmed. Rebecca bolts toward her grandmother's open arms. Reimer senses something: a prickling from Andie. This is not new. One day he hopes to have the energy to discuss it.

Doris serves them coffee and there's lemonade for Rebecca.

"I'll start on that eavestrough now," Reimer says, after eating two of Doris's just-baked double chocolate cookies. Minor maintenance is his end of their exchange for free babysitting.

"It's leaking at the joint above the front door," she says, "and, if you have time, I've noticed a few weak boards in the deck."

"No problem," he says, licking a crumb off his hand.

The afternoon pours on. He's glad for the sun, for the hammer, solid in his hands, and the fumes when he pries open a can of stain. Rebecca is back and forth between them, as if making sure they are all in their proper places. She brings him a third cookie. Her hands stick. They wash them with water from the garden hose.

"Will you stay for dinner?" Doris asks.

"No thanks," Reimer says, wiping his hands on his pants. "We're going to take advantage of the night alone, starting with dinner out."

"We should have left already," Andie says. "Mother, do you mind?"

Doris makes a whisking motion with her hands. "Go ahead, you've done enough —"

Rebecca whines. "I wanna come."

"Don't worry, we won't go to McDonald's without you," Andie says, bending to her daughter's height for a farewell hug.

"Promise?"

"Promise. Now be good for Grandma," Andie says. "We'll see you tomorrow afternoon . . . and we'll have a surprise for you."

"What surprise?"

"Well . . . we can't tell you." Andie runs her hand through her daughter's hair. "Or it wouldn't be a surprise, now, would it?"

In the car, Reimer asks, "What's the surprise?"

"We're changing her room."

"What?"

"Everything. The walls, sheets, the arrangement of the furniture. All of it."

"When did you decide this?" He speeds through a yellow light. A bus driver honks.

"Today. Just now. The stores are open for another three hours."

"Okay," Reimer says. And who's going to pay for this? Why didn't we discuss it first? He turns the radio on and lets someone else's voice take over when he knows he should have more to say.

ჼჼჼ

Andie has job interviews but no luck. Reimer wonders how long her confidence will hold out. Each morning she changes her outfit, her shoes, her earrings three times before she leaves. She can't make decisions about even the most trivial things: the grocery list, which radio station they should listen to. He tries to create a special place for her after his long hours at the office, a time to talk about her day. Andie has come to expect this attention from him, but most nights he's so exhausted after they've read to Rebecca and tucked her in, he hears only a fraction of their conversations.

"I said, she seems to be doing better."

They have switched topics. Or had they even been speaking? He doesn't know. The television is blaring. "Yes, she doesn't seem to miss the fish." How he needs sleep. Hours of it, days, a month. He needs the cerulean sky and a warm breeze. The smell of coconut oil and the little black boys who play stickball in the street and call him Mister. "Changing the room was a good idea."

A desk, stocked with crayons, paper and paints, fills the space where the aquarium had been. There's an easel, a bulletin board. Everywhere the girl turns, an opportunity to exorcise her fears. Her room is coral now, like the inside of a shell. There are no more nightmares, at least nothing she shares. Some nights Reimer stands in Rebecca's doorway after Andie goes to bed. Their daughter is restless, as though she suffers through sleep, but she doesn't wake. If only the dreams had been about something he could rationalize, a big bad wolf or a playground bully. The aquarium was an unlikely source; she'd had it a full year before the dreams. What the hell had shaken her?

❧❧❧

A month dissolves and Rebecca begins kindergarten. At first she clings to their legs when they drop her off, but she likes the routine of packing her backpack with a snack and finding something for Show and Tell. She takes their wedding photo. Pete the polar bear. Her good white shoes with the bows.

"She's scattered," Reimer concludes.

"Adjusting," Andie counters.

Reimer struggles to stay on track. At work he falls asleep over the thin blue lines that swim before his eyes. What do they mean? He no longer knows. His supervisor calls him in: there have been complaints. He needs to "shape up." To start pulling his weight. Reimer visualizes hauling a sleigh piled high with skin, bones and guts up a very long hill. There's his heel. An elbow. His weight.

હળહળ

Sand crabs scuttle from their shelters.

"Here," Andie says, dropping her armload of towels and beach toys. Reimer follows with the picnic basket and sun umbrella. His hands move in slow motion as he undoes a snap on the umbrella, then stabs it deep into the sand. Now he's under water. The umbrella becomes a spear gun, the sand pail a barracuda twisting to be free. He drops the spear gun and the fish darts off. As he breaks the water's surface, he finds himself buried to his neck in sand. Andie and Rebecca have made a moat around his head. The sun is relentless. He burns.

હળહળ

Andie startles when the phone rings. "Jesus . . . it's the middle of the night."

Reimer reaches for the phone. "Hello."

"Reimer, I'm sorry to wake you." It's Doris. She's breathless, but there's more: a catch in her voice, the beginning of something. He feels it in the cellar of his stomach.

"What's wrong?"

"Check Rebecca. I've had a bad dream. Just tell me that she's safe . . . and wake her."

He's afraid to move or make any sound that will confirm his own consciousness.

"Do it now!"

97

"Hold on." He throws the receiver to Andie, slips from the sheets, flicks the hall light on. Rebecca's room. Her chest rises in and out. She's warm to his touch. He shakes her. She moans and her eyelids flutter open. "It's okay, Princess, Daddy's just covering you up." He tucks her arms beneath the blankets and pulls them to her chin. "Go back to sleep."

Andie's on the phone. "He's here." She passes him the receiver.

"She's sleeping like a baby. What's go — "

"It was just so strong this time, I — "

"*This* time?" He raises his voice. "Doris, what are you talking about?"

Andie jerks the phone away. "I'll talk to him, Mom. Go back to sleep." She hangs up.

"What the fuck was that all about?"

She moves to the window and stares into the night like there is something important to see, something more than a few other squares of light and vague shapes moving inside them. "I didn't want to tell you. I thought it would . . . I don't know . . . go away."

He grabs her shoulder, spinning her, and sees the trail of yesterday's mascara on her cheeks.

"I thought it was over."

"You thought *what* was over?" Waves are crashing, but it's blood, not water, pounding against his temples.

"Mom's been having bad dreams about Becka for a long time. Frightening dreams. They're — they're Rebecca's dreams of water . . . weeds. Reimer — " she sucks her breath in through her teeth, "Mom sees her drowning."

Drowning. The undertow pulling them forever away. "How long have you known?"

She doesn't answer.

His fingers dig into her skin. "Tell me: how long have you known?"

She says nothing, and nothing, he thinks, could be worse.

ڡڡڡ

The file folders pile up — three, four, seven — on Reimer's desk. His mind needs an anchor; it keeps floating. This morning his supervisor slammed him for an incomplete project. He's called in sick twice since Doris's call. Secretaries whisper in the coffee room. There are no safe hours.

He tries again to focus on the blueprints mapped before him. *She didn't tell me. Why didn't she tell me?*

ڡڡڡ

Andie is hired at a hospital, across the city from where Rebecca was born. She likes it, likes making money and friends, while he feels more and more like a tourist in his own life. He insisted they register Rebecca in the daycare that operates out of her school. Andie didn't disagree. He's still awkward around his mother-in-law. He doesn't want to know about the murky, amphibious realm where she claims to have journeyed with his daughter.

ڡڡڡ

Rebecca's dreams stop just as they started. Without warning. She will be six in three weeks and they look upon the birthday as they would an artist's fresh canvas, a writer's *tabula rasa*. Perhaps this time they'll get it right. When the candles are blown out there'll be grown-up wishes in the air.

Reimer medicates his other world, but some nights it refuses obliteration. Then he smells the coconut oil and hears the smashing surf. His skin is bronzed, warm to the touch, and he speaks with another tongue. Waves explode against the wooden walls of his beachhouse and he feels it, ever so slightly, shift.

JEOPARDY

ALEX TREBEK IS JUST ABOUT TO READ THE FINAL *JEOPARDY!*
answer when the phone screws up everything. She forgot
to take it off the damn hook again, Wagner thinks, the
balloons of his lungs filling for an adequate sigh.

There it goes, Luanne muses, glancing at the door as if
the almost sexual aura of competition zinging around their
kitchen for the last twenty-five minutes possesses legs and
has left the room.

Neither responds to the noisy intrusion: they've earned
twelve points each and this last question could break the
tie.

The phone jangles again. Another ring and the machine
will kick in, but it might be important: one of the children,
needing them. Their oldest plays football and Luanne's felt
uneasy about it ever since she signed the medical waiver.
"Hello," she says, her voice flat with reluctance.

"Is Wagner there?" A woman's voice. Youngish, with a
little smoke in it. Luanne hands Wagner the receiver and
tries to speed-read the game show answer — on world
capitals — before it flashes off the screen. The TV — a
fourteen-inch colour set with a hanger attached to the
antenna — sits in the sticky dust on top of the fridge like
a small square head.

"Kristen?" Wagner's voice trills to the top of his scale. Almost a squeak. "Who is this?"

Luanne's missed the *Jeopardy!* answer — and the winning contestant's corresponding question. World capitals; hey, she might have had a chance.

"Who is this?" Wagner repeats, annoying her. "Kristen who?"

It's all lost now. Luanne adjusts the volume — news will be on soon, no need to blast those tragedies through the house — and watches her husband's expression become that of someone breathing a particularly offensive odour. Outdoor biffy, or meat that's fallen behind the freezer and remains undiscovered for a week. (She'll never live *that* one down.)

"I–I don't think so." His forehead has a slight sheen to it, and, Luanne's noticed, it's been getting higher and higher these last few years. It puckers into three neat folds when he's distressed. "I'm sure that . . . "

Must be a persistent telephone solicitor asking to clean their carpets. Maybe someone from the Firefighter's charity wanting them to sponsor poor kids for a circus, Luanne guesses. Those people always call when it's most inconvenient.

Wagner's winding up. "No, I don't think so." Then: "Goodbye."

"Who was that?" Luanne asks, lifting the receiver from the claw of his hand when he doesn't let go.

"Couldn't tell ya," he says, and an unprecedented fourth wrinkle appears. He turns away from her, takes a clean glass from the dishwasher, runs the tap for water. "Don't have a dingdang clue."

❧❧❧

When Derek arrives home from practice — famished, as usual, and sore (he's been rocked, twice) — he finds his parents puzzling over the mystery phone call.

"What exactly did she say?"

"She asked for your dad by name," Luanne says, remembering only now that she's defrosted ground beef and will have to whip up a disguise for supper. It doesn't matter what she concocts: Robyn won't eat it. Their daughter wrote a school report on the Ecoli virus last year and she's been on a mission to eliminate hamburger from the family menu ever since.

Wagner doesn't know whether to laugh or be upset about the call. "She said, 'I think you're really sexy.'" He shoots a look at Luanne for permission to proceed. She gives the slightest nod. "She said, 'I want to . . . fuck you.'" He's breathless, as if he's the one who's been tackled by a 230-pound linebacker.

"Get out. She said *that*! She wanted to *fuck* you? Holy shit!" Derek thinks this is the coolest thing that's ever happened to his father. "What'd you say?"

"He just kept asking who it was," Luanne interjects. "She sounded young." The hamburger's crackling on the skillet. She's decided on chili. "She said, 'I think you're really sexy,' twice, and she asked if he wanted to have an affair. When your dad said no, she asked 'Are you sure?'"

"Did you star 69 her?" Derek's cheeks are still blushed with energy left over from football practice. He hasn't taken his jacket off yet.

"No," Wagner says, a small tsunami pushing heat through his veins.

Sixty-nine. She'd said something about that, too.

Derek punches in the code and grabs a pencil. "No luck. She must have blocked the call."

The twins burst through the back door and the story is repeated for the thirteen year olds, minus expletives. "Go Dad!" Brent cheers, and raises his arm for a high-five. Wagner ignores him.

Robyn's steaming. She sinks into her mother — they're almost the same height — and folds thin arms around her shoulders. Thinks: that horny grade eight bitch!

After dinner the family flies in five directions: Luanne takes the sheltie for a walk; Wagner disappears downstairs to pound something in his workshop; Derek calls his girlfriend on the cordless phone; it's Brent's turn to do dishes (okay, *he* doesn't fly); Robyn stomps into the garden with her mother's sewing scissors. She squats beside the pansies, snips off their winsome faces, begins to plot revenge.

❧❧❧

Wagner awakes feeling refreshed, but before he scrunches back the sheets he remembers. The call. It'll make a good story at the office, he decides. Everyone will laugh.

"You still have no idea who that could have been?" Luanne's also awake, eyes fixed on the raisined bodies of six dead flies in the light fixture above the bed.

"None. Probably a wrong number," he says, though in his secret heart he wants the tease of intent. Hell, he'll be forty-four on his next birthday. And he's hardly grey at all. He feels good. In fact, he might even do a few sit-ups this morning, get the old juice pumping. My God, he thinks, stretching his calf muscles, it's a bloody great day to be alive.

"Well, I hope so." Luanne pulls her knees toward her waist then swings them to the left, as if she's doing a warm-up before an aerobics class. "I've got to get up." She has a half day at an elementary school on the east side. She knows the principal, generally likes the other staff, can't stand most of the older students. It's always the same — a nervousness that begins in her throat, snails around her stomach then quickly heads south to her bowels. She bolts to the ensuite toilet, makes it just in time. They never let her forget she's a substitute teacher: a sub. The word makes her think of sinking.

She hollers at Wagner — still in bed, listening to CBC — to get the kids up. In the mirror she pushes her newly permed hair back and examines her profile from both angles. She lifts her eyelids with her thumbs, then stretches the skin at her temples up and back, making herself cat-eyed. Do I look old? she wonders. Would anyone call to beg sex from me?

She steps into the shower. The first pellets of water feel like marble-sized hail on her head. The rotten egg smell of her perm lingers on; a toxic taste at the back of her tongue. Could the call have been a prank? Kids playing "Truth or Dare," like she and her girlfriends might have when they were young and eager for trouble's infallible thrill, although they'd never have stooped to these depths.

Or maybe call girls are recruiting new johns via phone sex. Hard times are everywhere, it seems.

She shampoos and rinses, conditions and rinses. The shower's steamed up the mirror. She drags a finger through the condensation, and when Wagner edges past her, he sees it there: a giant question mark splitting his reflection.

❧❧❧❧

They're unlocking the front door when the next call comes.

They've been to an all-you-can-eat restaurant — for a treat; Wagner thought they could use one. Brent sprints toward the phone, leaving a muddy story across the hardwood. "I'll get it!"

"Your shoes!" Luanne calls after him. She's been trying to train her family; it's hard enough with the dog tracking the outdoors in every day. More work awaits.

"For you, Dad-o!"

Luanne arranges shoes tossed carelessly across the porch: Derek's cleats and runners; Brent's "skater" shoes; Robyn's black wedges (which Luanne thinks inappropriate for a girl her age). She'll have to get a wet, soapy rag and wipe the floor. Only Wagner's managed to set his shoes — practical brown leather casuals which go from home to office — on the shelf, but it's he who angers her most. That look he's wearing these days, like he's not sure what to do with his mouth, where to fix his eyes. Smug bastard.

She finds her family in the kitchen, and with one glance at Wagner she knows it's happened again. "It was her," he says, matter-of-factly.

"What'd she say this time?" Brent's almost panting.

"The same thing, basically," Wagner says, "until I hung up on her."

"Let's star 69 her," Derek offers, then, realizing the innuendo in that number, he chuckles as he pushes the buttons.

What the hell is this? Luanne wonders. Isn't anyone rooting for me?

The five of them wait for Derek's verdict: "No luck again."

"Once may have been an accident, even funny," Luanne hears herself saying, "but this is not a joke anymore. I'm calling SaskTel. Robyn, would you bring me the book please? It's downstairs."

"What's it doing down there?" Wagner asks.

Robyn disappears. "Kristen," my ass. Trust Candace to do something like this, she thinks. So Jon kissed me and she thought they were still going out, big deal. *This* is low.

Derek opens the fridge and gawks inside. Bowls and jars clink as he moves them around, trying to find the good stuff at the back.

"For crying out loud, we just ate!" Wagner closes the door on his son, who, at seventeen, has already grown taller and broader than his father. Bet he thinks he can take me, too, Wagner guesses, hoping they'll never have to find out.

"What'll you tell the phone company, Lu?"

"Nothing," she says, after Robyn reappears with the directory. "It's your problem." She pushes the book into his chest. "Deal with it."

Wagner finds the pages listing the telephone company's myriad departments. He wonders which to call for suggestive phone calls. It wasn't exactly obscene: there'd been no heavy breathing, and it didn't even upset him that much, truth be known. He dials the number for residential service and explains his plight. The ethereal voice on the other end puts him on hold. The call's transferred, and he repeats his story to a man named Franco. As he's telling it, the whole thing feels surreal, as if he's outside of all this — these events are happening to another man, standing in some other kitchen with some other family ringed around him as if hungry for a stoning.

Wagner thinks he hears Franco guffaw.

"I'm sorry? Did you say something?" he asks. He doesn't relish not being taken seriously, but Franco says they'll investigate and get back to him ASAP.

"Well, that's that." Wagner sets the directory beneath the phone. Someone's given all the pretty faces on the cover blue beards, devil's horns, inky teeth and Mohawks. "That's all we can do for now."

"When you find out who it is, can you sue?" Brent asks, flipping his sandy hair out of his eyes. He's the family capitalist. He's contracted out several of his grass-mowing jobs to neighbouring nine and ten year olds, paying them forty percent to his sixty. He knows about things like Pacific Rim funds and stock splitting.

"Don't you have homework or something?" Robyn asks. She inspects her bare foot. An ugly, nickel-sized blister has formed on her left heel from the new shoes. Candace has the same pair and accused her of copycatting. As if!

"Mom, where are the bandages?"

Luanne opens the junk drawer and stirs around. "Check my bathroom." My? No one notices the possessive slip except Luanne herself. "Derek, what's up for you tonight?"

"Going to Tanya's," he says. "She rented a movie. Some Julia Roberts chick flick, probably."

"You have homework?" Wagner asks. He's opened the newspaper to the daily crossword. Luanne, he sees, has beat him to it.

"A few questions in math, but don't worry, if there's bawling chicks, I'll be back before the first tear falls."

The children scatter, leaving Wagner and Luanne and the sheltie, Alex (after Trebek), who's not supposed to be in the kitchen, and knows it. "I didn't want to say anything in front of the kids," Wagner casually begins, "but there was more. She was explicit this time."

"Explicit? What do you mean explicit? What'd she say?" Oh, she could shake him right now. Rattle his bones like he's rattled her nerves.

"She said she wanted to . . . said she'd — "

"Never mind," Luanne's head is doing loop-de-loops. "I'm sure it was scintillating. You must be flattered. Most guys have to pay $4.99 per minute for that kind of talk."

"Are you mad at me?" Wagner asks. "You sound like you're really mad at me!"

Luanne picks up the dishcloth and soaks it beneath the tap. She crocheted the damn thing herself; what a martyr, she thinks. Anyone else would just fork over two bucks at Wal-Mart, but not her; oh, no, she has to do everything the hard way. Who the hell even noticed all the effort she put into keeping the ship of this household afloat?

She scrubs the counter so hard it could be considered assault. It's already clean. "Of course I'm not mad. Why would I be mad?"

"It's ridiculous to be mad. There's nothing to be mad about. You act like I'm enjoying this, like I instigated it or something!"

"Well."

"Well?" He's standing with his short legs slightly spread, his palms open and facing her.

She has the disconsolate, little-girl feeling of being scolded, for the first time by someone other than a parent or teacher.

Wagner says, "I'm going to cut the grass."

Luanne watches him march outside in his sock feet.

"My shoes," he says, stepping back in. He's not a good fighter. Fighting really throws him. His words tangle up like carpet fringes in the vacuum cleaner. He even has trouble reprimanding the kids; the twins positively undo him.

"You wanna do something, Mom?"

It's Robyn. Has she heard all that? Luanne wonders. She's either made a mess of her mascara or she's been crying. It's the age, Luanne believes.

There's been some kind of trouble with other girls in her class. Hell hath no fury like a schoolgirl clique. Robyn won't speak of it.

"Sure, honey. Anything on TV tonight? Maybe we can watch something together." She reaches to rest her hand on Robyn's shoulder. The phone rings. Mother and daughter freeze. "I'll get it," Luanne says.

Robyn clenches her teeth. Candace flat out, freaking denied it. Well, if it really wasn't her, it was Erika, she decides. Erika's had it in for her ever since she was the only grade fiver not invited to Robyn's birthday party. She should have answered. She'd recognize the voice. Then it'd be party over.

"The phone company," Luanne whispers over her hand.

They've traced the number to a downtown payphone. Luanne thanks them, says she'll tell her husband and they'll decide whether or not to get an unlisted number.

"Too strange," Robyn says, after Luanne hangs up. She has a hard time meeting her mother's eyes. "There's zip on TV. How about helping me change my room around?"

"Sure." Luanne rubs her stomach above her belt. She's uncomfortably full from the meal: mostly Chinese food with too much MSG. She always overeats at all-you-can-eat restaurants. Whole hog, Brent calls it. They all go whole hog, except Robyn, who picks at her food as if it's contaminated. Damn, Luanne thinks. Why can't I be one of those women who knows when to stop, who doesn't go back for a second dessert, with soft ice cream swirled into a leaning tower on the side, a liberal topping of caramel and peanuts? Does the girl behind the phone call have willpower, she wonders?

In the bedroom she unzips her jeans and pulls on one of Wagner's green Saskatchewan Roughrider sweatshirts to cover her bloated belly. She hears drawers being wrenched open in the next room.

"Come on, Mom!"

Robyn's bedroom is a disaster, but instead of tidying it, her solution is to "change it around" every six months or so, a job which necessitates her mother's help.

"So," Luanne says, surveying the landscape of twisted bedding, dirty clothes (a black bra? Luanne's never even owned one), stuffed animals, make-up and movie star posters that have escaped their posts on the wall, "where should we begin?"

᭥᭥᭥

Wagner's having trouble with the lawnmower, an electric he picked up at a yard sale for twenty-five bucks. Luanne warned him about buying anything electrical second-hand. "There's a reason why they're selling it," she'd said. "It'll be more trouble than it's worth." It wasn't the machine as much as the fifteen-metre electrical cord: he'd had to bind it with black tape and now it keeps coming unplugged from the machine. He feels like he's being watched, like his neighbours are laughing at his incompetence. He ties the cord to the handle. This will be the last mowing of the year.

"Need some help, Dad?" Brent's sitting on the front step, sucking a blue Mr. Freeze.

"Yes, could you finish this up for me?"

"Three bucks?"

"Come on. You live here. I've paid for your whole life."

Brent tilts his head and squeezes the last of the Mr. Freeze — now a watery drink — into his mouth. "Two fifty?"

Wagner wonders how they've raised this child, how it's progressed this far. "Two bucks, and that includes the boulevard." He marches up the front steps and throws questions from the doorway while he slips off his shoes. "Did they call back? Lu? Did anyone call?"

Luanne comes halfway down the stairs. She's been sweating, and her hair's a melodrama pasted to her neck. She expects that she smells badly. And so what? "She — your secret admirer with the potty mouth — called from a phone booth. Down on Second Avenue."

"Oh." It's all he can think to say.

❧❧❧

Suddenly it's late October. Stores wear garlands of orange and black, Clinton and Lewinsky masks fly off the shelves. There've been no calls for a month.

Luanne stands at her back door, appraising the autumn garden. The patio umbrella remains canopied over the table; late-blooming petunias dot the garden in pink. It's quiet, with the kids in school, Wagner at work. She has these hours for herself.

I could be doing anything, she realizes, and glances at the novel left on the counter. She's been trying to stay on top of the CanLit scene, but the last three books she's read have been too intelligent, too witty, too hip. Urbane books by single, male Torontonians in their mid-thirties whose hip, urbane, single, male characters (the odd woman with great tits, designer clothes and killer dialogue is occasionally thrown in) wax poetic over which Chardonnay to order. Like *that's* life!

She thinks about each of her children. Derek has a part-time job at a bowling alley; Brent has his hands full managing his team of eavestrough cleaners and lawn rakers. And Robyn. She's come through the rough patch — nothing she'd talk about — but just before Thanksgiving she became pretty and popular in the same moment. Luanne smiles toward the lilac at the back of the yard. Robyn's taking a course at the YWCA and earning her babysitting certificate. There's another black bra in her dresser, with wire push-ups, and crescent moons of foam that slip into the lining. It happens so fast, Luanne thinks, though she's happy her family's growing older. And Wagner says he is, too.

She calls him at the office, suggests he leave work early. "I've washed the sheets," she purrs self-consciously, trying to sound sultry. It's a joke between them. Back when they were having regular sex — before their children became so aware — it seemed they always made love after she'd just washed the sheets. Every other day dwindled to once a week; then, a few times a month. Always it was quiet — the children might hear something, and know—and controlled, and not particlarly satisfying. Plus, they were beat.

"I can be there in twenty minutes," Wagner says, trying not to sound too surprised or too eager — too *anything* — lest she change her mind.

After, they drift off in the room's wash of buttery sunlight.

The phone rings.

"Are you getting that?" Wagner mumbles into his pillow. The phone is on Luanne's side of the bed.

"Nope. Let it ring." She tucks her knees into the backs of Wagner's and throws her arm across him. She likes to sleep skin to skin, and they so rarely get to. Through the closed and locked door — they can't be too careful: Derek might get out early, one of the twins might come home sick — they hear the answering machine's loud tone, a woman's message being recorded.

Luanne tosses. Wagner's fallen into the rhythmic breathing of deep sleep. She slides away, pulls on her terry housecoat.

"Hi, Wagner. It's Kristen. Been a long time. My offer's still open . . . and so are my legs. Are you ready for me? Are you ready to fuck me, Wagner?"

Luanne yanks the cassette from the machine. Anyone could have heard that — Brent, Robyn, guests, anyone. She grabs a knife from its wall mount and cracks the tape apart. Brent finds her propped against the counter, ribbons of tape looped across the linoleum and her rag doll legs.

"I'll get Dad," he says.

❧❧❧

So frustrating! Not Candace, not Erika, then who? Robyn makes two lists: in one column, all the girls who hate her. In the other, any girls she's brought home, anyone who has even *hinted* that her dad looks kind of hot for his age. Lisa?

No. She doesn't have the guts. Shanae? Nope — that chick can't keep a secret.

She scribbles and scratches, deliberates some more. I'll get to the bottom of this, she thinks, if it takes all flippin' year.

જ✥જ✥જ✥

"Tell me you have no idea who this is. Swear to me!"

They've gone for a drive in the country and have ended up at an approach facing a field. Only dirt remains. The sun's setting crimson, signalling another warm day to follow. Luanne hasn't packed away the summer clothes yet. She's still wearing sandals.

"I swear. Damn it to hell, Lu! Give me some credit here." Wagner's hunched forward, both hands on the wheel, as if manoeuvering through a storm, though the minivan's been parked more than an hour.

"How does she know you're married? She always uses the word 'affair.'"

"I don't know, lucky guess, I suppose. Anyway, she won't be calling again. The new number's unlisted."

He has no idea how close she is. No idea. The images that are kaleidoscoping through her head. She suspects everyone: his coworkers, bank tellers, even Derek's exgirl-friend, Tanya. Wagner always joked around with her; there was a certain familiarity between them. Tanya's an attractive gal, with long reddish-brown hair and muscular legs, like one of those Irish step dancers.

Luanne's pout extends across the breadth of her face. "I feel like walking."

"What, here? You can't be serious. It's getting dark . . . we're miles from . . . what if a car comes?"

But she's gone. Off and running down the backbone of highway, east, away from the city's pinprick lights that are growing brighter as the sky darkens.

She kicks off one sandal, tries to free the other. She hops and struggles to unbuckle at the same time: too difficult. She abandons the sandal and resumes her clumsy pace. The pavement's cold beneath her one bare foot. The van's engine turns over, gravel spits and crunches as Wagner leaves the approach. He's on the highway now. Right behind her.

She thinks about *Jeopardy!* Slutty women who come on to conceivably innocent, middle-aged men, for five hundred, Alex. She's a woman watching a woman who looks a lot like herself, on the TV with the buggered up antenna. She's waiting to see what will happen next.

AVENIDA TRISTE

IT'S THE FIRST DAY HE KNOWS WITH CRYSTAL CERTAINTY THAT
the sun's not just teasing, she's slipped into her summer
dress for the duration. Caramel-winged butterflies flit against
white fences. Sparrows, robins and birds he's yet to learn
names for dart between crabapple trees. He can almost
smell the lilacs' purple impatience in his own back yard as
he walks the two kilometres from the nursing home.

It's the season, exploding. Sam fills his lungs with it.

His front door is unlocked. "I'm home," he announces,
more to himself than to Eden. She knows the door's
supposed to stay locked, even during the afternoon.
Whelan, their neighbour to the south, has lost three bikes
in the last month from his verandah. His insurance
premiums are out of this world.

"Back here," Eden calls. He follows the thread of her
voice to the patio, finds her sprawled across two deck
chairs, eyes closed, one foot bobbing. There's music: a song
from the 1960s with a hum-along tune. The patio umbrella
blocks sun from Eden's face but the light hits her long, bare
legs squarely. She has pledged to avoid full facial sun this
year, fears premature aging more than skin cancer. Her
breasts are squeezed into a black bikini top and lifted to
unnatural heights; skin so presently pale it appears to glow,

but by the end of the season she's as copper-toned as any California girl.

Sam slides into a chair, appraises the other view. The yard is mostly mud, generously gouged wherever Eden's mother's collie felt the urge to dig: they dog-sat while Marlene was in Weslaco, Texas. He wonders how many bulbs he's lost. Yesterday he counted forty-nine debutante tulips and scratched this fact into the notebook he'd labelled — in a generous, early, double entendre — The Garden of Eden. The first crocus pushed through today.

He's divided the rectangular lot into four sections, but swerved his flagstone path so the divisions are obscured. From the second floor sunroom, the path takes the shape of a dancing woman. A small continent of ice floats in the pond's brackish water. No fish yet. He's flushed two; the remaining eight goldfish are literally dying to get out of the basement bathtub he's wintered them in. He'll err on the safe side, give the fish another two weeks.

Behind him, the north fence has been partly scraped. An open can of exterior latex lies thick and abandoned on newspaper. "I was going to ask what was new but I see that your day hasn't been a total write-off." He stares at Eden's bare feet. "You've painted your toenails."

Eden stretches, points her toes like a diver. "Cameo Creme. You like?"

"Marvy."

She scales him with her eyes. Sometimes he thinks she was a cat in another life. Sometimes she pretends the same. She has that sense about her, that ability to stare down another person, eyes unwavering, her thoughts imperceptible, though they've been together seven years, time he measures in seed catalogues, gardening magazines, how they've stretched up and up the closet wall.

"You want a drink or something?" Sam scrapes his chair back. Inside he grabs two cans of Labatt Lite from the fridge door. The house smells like it's curdling. He sniffs the garbage. Nothing. An olfactory mystery that reappears every few months. "So?" He sets the bottles on the patio table.

Eden's eyes remain closed. "So."

"Where's the paper?"

She points to the paint can. The lid is stuck to the classifieds. Sam pries it off, tearing a section of newsprint. He holds the paper up, peers through the hole.

"I did the cryptoquip already," she says.

"You finish it?"

"No." She had hoped that her university degree would at least give her that: the edge on the daily cryptoquip. *O* equals *R*, *B* equals *C*. How hard could that be? That she gave up a pleasant job with SaskEnergy in order to fill the gaps in her history degree and came out the other end with a $17,000 debt, a diploma on which her name is misspelled, and no promise of any job has left her feeling, on a good day, used. On a bad day she avoids walking across bridges. She thinks the only thing worse than being unemployed would be to be old and unemployed.

Sam doesn't want much, or so he's told Adrienne, the amiable divorcee from Vancouver who bought the house beside his and has become his new best friend. "To be able to pay the bills, enjoy the odd vacation, watch my garden grow."

But there's more. Always more, swimming just below the surface, like an algae eater. In Sam's case it's more a matter of what might not be swimming. He fears a virtual absence of sperm. He began to suspect when Valerie, his partner before Eden, regularly neglected her birth controls pill without incident. Near the end she went off them altogether. They split and she was pregnant within months. It's not that he yearns to be a father, he just wants the option. His brother has two healthy boys and another child on the way. His sister, a pair of golden-haired girls. His anxiety has been a wolf in a cage for too many years: pacing, pacing. Just the option. That's all he wants.

Three weeks earlier he talked himself into sharing his concern at his annual physical; the GP suggested they find out for sure. The result: Azoospermia. Sam thought it sounded like a small marine animal with sharp teeth. One of those Slang Teaser words you make up a definition for. Was there a blockage? The doctor offered him a small dish of hope. There'd been more tests. Waiting. Eden doesn't know. The final call is yet to come.

ଏଏଏଏ

Saturday evening, Eden is at her mother's. Sam was welcome to join them for spaghetti and meatballs, but lately Marlene's been too prickly for his taste, says — to their faces — that it's "about damn time" they either wrapped up their lengthy relationship or tied it into a nuptial knot. "Forget the church," she asserted last time they met, though she'd dreamt of losing fifteen pounds and dazzling her ex in a saucy, peach-coloured mother-of-the-bride number, "I've got the JP's number in my head."

Yet they balk. And although the present excuse is Eden's lack of work, neither she nor Sam can shape their real hesitations into a satisfactory speech. So what? "No one gets married anymore," Eden tells Marlene as she twists the rubbery noodles around a fork. The collie's head rests heavily on her thigh. When Marlene puts water on for tea, Eden slips the dog a treat.

"I saw that," Marlene says from the sink.

Eden stares at her mother's back. "How do you do that?"

"Intuition. You'll get it, too . . . when you're a mother yourself." Her voice slides along the walls.

"Ma, you're pushing again. I've already told you, I want to be more than a wife, a mother. I don't want a man or a child to define who I am. I want to be somebody. I *will* be somebody."

"Are you suggesting that I'm nobody?" Marlene has returned to her food. She stops sawing a meatball.

"No, Ma, I'm not saying that. It's just . . . remember when I was little and Dad used to tell me I could be anything I wanted? Well, I believed him. He had me convinced that if I wanted to be the first woman on the moon or the queen of bloody Sheba or the next Betty Friedan, all I had to do was work hard and it would happen. Here's the last three jobs I've applied for — ." She readies her fingers for counting," — a courier for small packages, a labourer at the university's research farm, a receptionist at a large wholesale firm. See? It's not happening, damn it. It's not fucking happening!"

Marlene dabs her mouth with her napkin. Such a tongue on that girl. "Who is Betty Friedan?"

"Mother!"

Marlene stands. "I made a cake," she says. "I'm getting it now."

ೋೋೋ

Sam is in Adrienne's back yard, bent over the weekend crossword. "A six-letter word for indifference," he reads. "Starts with A."

Adrienne hasn't heard. She's still inside, filling a second bowl of beer nuts. Sam sets the puzzle aside. The sun is hot but dying; the beer cold. He enjoys viewing his garden from this perspective. His lilacs have filled out nicely and it appears his white rose has survived the collie's abuse. "Miracle," he says to the new leaves.

"What's that?" Adrienne sets the beer nuts between them. She has, he notices, strong hands. Gardener's hands. He feels very close to her.

"Nothing important." He scoops some nuts. They are slightly sticky. "No mosquitoes yet."

"Don't bother me much anyway," she says, tucking a muscled calf beneath her. She's a speed walker. Six miles a day. "Never have."

Her grey Persian, Tinker's Damn, or Tink, for short, springs into her lap. The cat's the one thing Sam regrets about his neighbour. He expects that Tink (like all the other neighbourhood cats) is going to shit in his annuals. A coworker swears by dry cat food, says he should sprinkle it in his beds. "They won't shit where they eat." He's going to try it. "Lucky you. Mosquitoes devour me. And I welt." He mimes a huge lump on his arm and Adrienne laughs.

"So's there been any action at the drug house lately?" She pops a beer nut into her mouth.

He knows she's concerned about the goings-on in the brick rental house across the street. The top floor tenants have a thriving drug trafficking operation. An intermittent convoy of vehicles stops at all hours: horns honk and the hockey-haired drug dealer — spikes on top, long, oily strands in back — comes out to deal. "Just the usual."

Adrienne scoots Tink, pinches a cat hair off her shorts. "The other night they were chasing each other around with hatchets. High as kites, as usual. Honestly," she shakes her head, "there are little kids on the block."

"Did you call the cops?"

"Not yet," she says. "And that guy with the long hair, he's always hanging out his window, staring at everyone. I've quit using my front door."

Funny, Sam thinks, Eden's home all day and she's never mentioned this. Is she that unaware? He imagines catcalls, pictures the greasy creep staring Eden down as she bends to move the sprinkler in her cut-off shorts. Who knows what the bastard's thinking? He would talk to her.

"And it's not just pot," Adrienne interjects. "I bet he's selling heroin, cocaine . . . the works. I mean, have you seen some of those guys?"

"It's the honking that pisses me off," Sam says. He's not opposed to taking the occasional toke himself, but that's where he draws the line. "It's so inconsiderate."

"The whole thing really bugs me," Adrienne says, her voice falling an octave. "We should do something."

"Yes," Sam agrees, finishing his third and final beer. He has transplanting to do. Wants to check his Roma tomatoes, started beneath fluorescent lights he hawked from the nursing home. A perk, he feels, for hoisting the babysoft flesh of seniors around all day. "We must."

❧❧❧

Sam jerks awake, thinks he has slept in. His heart settles when he realizes it's Friday: he's off. Ah, but there's something about this day, he thinks. What was it? Then he remembers: the doctor is calling.

He attempts a return to the world behind his eyes: a baptism, in a large church with intricate plaster angels, a pipe organ and giant stained glass windows. The sun shone crimson and royal blue behind the glass, emerald where a tree leafed through a Mary and Baby Jesus scene, but there was also a black snake, a bone-white skull, too many unexplained shadows. Sam faces the front. Two figures — the parents? — stand with their backs to the congregation as a minister draws the cross on their sleeping infant's head. The parents turn.

Strangers, like most characters who populate the cities of his dreams. The minister walks toward the congregation, cradling the baby. Those near the aisle lean forward, coo, touch a tiny hand as the pair pass. When the minister approaches Sam's pew, he reaches to touch the sleeping child. Cold. Plastic. The blond wisps of hair are painted on.

His nightmare is lost to two loud horn blasts. He stumbles to the window: a rusted El Camino at the rental house. The drug dealer climbs into the back seat. It's 7:24. "Prick." Sam scribbles the license number on a bank receipt.

Eden's asleep. She's been staying up late, watching old movies, allowing herself the luxury of waking at a civilized speed and hour. Sam loves the curve of her long neck, the exposed collarbones that suggest a vulnerability that doesn't manifest in her daytime character. With her dark hair now cut short, she could pass for twenty-five, easy. After she wakes, the realities of her stagnant world surface in a furrow between her eyes, and the weight of being thirty-two and unemployed crashes over her.

"I'm getting up," he says, slightly pissed off that even without the noise outside, his body never allows him to sleep past 7:30. "Looks nice out."

He's drawn to the sunroom window, the glory of his garden. The beds need some attention, and he's hoping to purchase a new pump for the pond, but coffee and the newspaper must come first. He opens his door just as the papergirl is coming up the walk. She's mostly hidden in an over-sized sweatshirt, but he guesses her to be about twelve. Pretty, he thinks, her face small as a pixie's, but hard not to notice the bony ankles below jeans that have two inches of darker denim stitched to the hem, the unfortunate running shoes — unglued from their soles and flapping like the mouth of a talking horse. "Hey," she says. Sam thinks he should say something, introduce himself, at least. She throws him a smile before she's off, pulling a squeaky red wagon stacked with papers.

"Was that the new kid?" Eden says, behind him. He turns. She's tied a housecoat over her undershirt and boxers.

"Yes. A girl this time." He waves the paper. "Why'd you get up?"

"Pigeons," she says, "cooing right outside our window. They do it on purpose."

"Paranoid already? It's not even eight." Sam takes his toast, coffee and newspaper outside to the patio. The sky holds promise, and there's just enough breeze to stir new leaves on the giant poplars that rise above his alley; a green oasis in the heart of the city. He hears Eden moving around the kitchen. In the morning's second surprise, she brings her Bran Flakes out and joins him. Her hair is mussed, eyes slightly theatrical with slept-in mascara.

"Mom laid it on pretty thick last night. I wish you'd have been there."

"What's her problem?" He feels a rising plug of anger. He doesn't understand this bandwagon; he's convinced the woman's never liked him, why would she want them to marry? "Can't find her own man so she has to live vicariously through her daughter's wedding? That's sick."

"It's just that . . . " Eden looks past him, to the spot that will fill with raspberries. "I'm her only kid. You know, her only chance for grandchildren and all that."

There, Sam thinks. She's said it. They've never talked much about kids, but there it is, the word waving right out in front of them like a white sheet on a clothesline. "You've never given a shit about kids before." He hides his eyes between newsprint headlines. Wars are raging everywhere.

"That's pretty crass," Eden says, "even for you. When did you become such an asshole?" Moments later she's whipping cutlery or something equally sharp and loud around the kitchen.

This is work, he thinks, imagining scars on the kitchen walls, knife wounds in the linoleum. "E-den . . . ," he calls in his best conciliatory voice, making her name a singsong, " . . . come out here."

The noises cease. She opens the back door and hovers on the threshold, queen-of-the-castle, five steps above him. "Why? It obviously doesn't matter to you. Just let me deal with it, as always. No skin off your ass. Nothing matters to you — "

He'd like to interrupt, cast a Shakespearean flourish toward the garden. He knows better. "It does matter. *You* matter. Look, we need to talk." A bloated robin lights on the empty bird feeder. Something else he must get to. Last year they had an American goldfinch and a ruby-throated kinglet in the yard. And are those aphids on the Virginia creeper? Already? He'll be damned if he's going to lose it again this year. "I'll marry you if you want."

"Well that's about as bloody romantic as I guess I can expect from a guy who gave me a ball glove for Valentine's Day." She pulls on a section of her hair, something she's been doing a lot of since she shucked a good foot of it off, as if she could stretch it back to its former length. Denial, he thinks. Phantom locks.

"Well?" He feels a fluttering, thinks it's his heart, touches there, then realizes a pigeon's swooped through the lilac behind him.

Eden is beside him. She quarter smiles. "I'll think about it."

Sam breathes. He had thought she wanted a ball glove.

He swallows the last of his drink, keeps his thoughts focused on spring, the garden, five sparrows telling tales on the power line. When the phone rings, he lunges toward it.

"There is an absence of production of mature sperm in the tubules of the two testes," the doctor says, delivering the news, the *non*-life sentence, Sam thinks, like an indifferent judge. "It's extremely rare."

"Of course it is," Sam answers, decoding the medical bullshit. *Now it's official: I'm shooting blanks.*

"Who was that on the phone?" Eden asks from the patio.

"Wrong number," he calls back, then whispers: "Someone looking for a man."

❧❧❧

The weather holds. Now, on his third day off, he's adding grass seed to the front lawn where the dog has left his mark.

He had tried dousing the yellowed areas with water and baking soda — something he'd heard on CBC radio — but it hasn't helped.

Adrienne wanders out in shorts and slippers and sits on her wide front step.

A lime-coloured tank top salutes the freckles on her shoulders.

"Hey, I thought you weren't using your front door anymore," he says.

"You're out here. I was hoping you'd protect me."

He laughs, wonders if she is flirting. She eyes the patchy grass. "Think it'll come back?"

"Oh, yeah. I'll water it to death, try to keep the neighbourhood kids off it." He continues scattering seed, his back to Adrienne now. He's shirtless. Eden once told him she liked him in blue jeans with his chest bare. He feels the light of Adrienne's eyes on him as he slowly backs across the lawn. There's no denying the current of possibility that hums between them, but there's Eden, and besides, what he needs most is a friend.

He spreads a last handful of seed, wipes his hands on the sides of his jeans, then takes the butter knife from his pocket and digs out the starfish-shaped beginnings of a dandelion. This used to be Eden's job, he remembers. Life used to be so simple with her. Strolling down the back alleys of Spadina or Saskatchewan Crescent, holding hands, peering through knot-holes in seven-foot fences to see the landscaped yards, swimming pools, tiered decks, and believing that this — prosperity, a few good friends gathered around a pool with tall drinks in their hands — was what was ahead of them. Eden believed it, too. Where did that go?

"Want some coffee?" Adrienne lifts her cup, pats the space beside her.

"Don't mind if I do." He tosses the knife onto his step and crosses the invisible green border between their yards.

She springs up. "I'll be right back."

A neighbour three houses to the north starts his van and drives off. Two springs ago, when the man was in the process of moving in, Sam asked if he was the fellow who'd bought the house. "Who wants to know?" the man asked, his arms hugging a stereo speaker. Sam's welcome was trapped in his throat. The new guy tore out his dogwood, nuked everything green, ripped up a yard with excellent potential and built a two-car garage. His front yard is gravel and white rock. Sam can't stand him.

"It's on the strong side," Adrienne says, handing him a large cup. "Hope that's okay."

"Perfect," he says, sipping. He casually moves his knee when she bumps it with her own.

"I'm going to split these tiger lilies in the fall," she says, pointing to her right. "Too bunched up." They inspect the still flowerless plants.

"They look like palm trees for Barbie dolls," he says. "Can I have a few for the back?"

"Sure. Swap you for some hosta. And maybe a few ferns. God, I love ferns."

Sam smiles inside. He loves ferns, too.

A neighbour's door opens and a bare arm stabs into the mailbox. Whelan steps out in his underwear, holding his newspaper, unaware or unashamed of the loose, candy-striped boxers. "See we're finally getting it at a decent time." He squints down the street. "They must've let that big slow kid go."

"I don't think he was slow," Adrienne says, "just looked like it . . . the way he skulked, head down like a dog who knows he's been bad. I hear there's something like fourteen kids in his family. I kinda felt sorry for him."

Sam doesn't feel particularly sorry. He helped to get the guy fired. Brought the paper hours after Sam was already at work, and occasionally they didn't get it at all. Plus, he never took the effort to push the paper right through the door slot. The neighbours took turns phoning the *StarPhoenix* to complain; discussing the incompetence of paper carriers had become a neighbourhood ritual. "Remember the kid before him?"

Whelan nods. "Kept stealing the paper money. I still suspect the little bugger snatched one of my bikes."

Adrienne turns. "Really?"

"Well," Whelan hitches his shorts, "wife wants to go yard saling . . . I'd better get dressed. Later."

"What'd you say he does for a living?" Adrienne asks when Whelan's safely inside. She's still learning the neighbourhood. Sam's been helping. After she moved in and immediately began clearing weeds, he dropped a "Welcome to the Neighbourhood" card in her mailbox. The card had a pansy design.

∾∾∾

Monday, last day off before seven on, and still so much to do.

He pours coffee, discovers the paper hasn't arrived. Both he and Eden slept fitfully. Sam suggests they finish painting the fence together. It has to be done before he puts the gladiola bulbs in, and before the wild rose and lilac bushes fill out even more. "You finish the scraping, I'll paint," he says, handing her one of his old flannel shirts to button over her bra. It's barely 9:00, but the temperature's already climbing and the sky's only promise is more heat. He's got to get some water on that lawn.

"Sure. Whatever," she snaps, taking the shirt and following him outside. "You're the boss."

The boss? "Eden, I don't know what's up your ass, but this is getting old already." He glances over his shoulder to make sure Adrienne doesn't have to hear this. Their other neighbour, a crop scientist and a provincial authority on wheat midge, has been at the lab for hours. "I'm sorry life after university is such a disappointment. I'm sorry that you haven't been able to find that stimulating, high salary job. I'm sorry for the goddamn weeds and your mother's constant bitching, but I can't keep putting up with this bullshit." His hands have been flying. He stuffs them in his pockets, rocks back on his heels, breathes two-three-four. "Life's too short. I work hard at a job I don't particularly like and when I come home bonebattered at the end of the day, the last thing I want to hear is you ragging on me." *Tell her! Give her the chance to bolt.*

Eden trembles uncharacteristically. "Well you don't know what it's like for me," she starts, tapping her breastbone. "My self-confidence is slipping away like, like . . . " she holds her hands out, palms up, " . . . like, shit, I don't know."

It's her soapbox now. He gives her that.

"I'm young, smart . . . pretty enough, wouldn't you say? Last week I was in a room with nine other women, all around my age. Ten hopefuls in navy dresses and practical haircuts, waiting our turns to be interviewed for a job as a receptionist! But that's not the worst. The worst was when we discovered in that entire group of women, I was the only one who's never been to New York."

Eden grabs the wire brush. He doesn't know whether to hold her or to duck. She's wrong about him. He does understand. Lately he's felt like an extra in the movie of his life. He focuses on what is wonderful: she never lets him go to sleep before kissing him, like a mother, on the cheek; she orchestrated his surprise thirtieth birthday party with a Latin theme, including a *piñata*, and music by Rubén Blades and Celia Cruz. She often sensed when his back needed rubbing; she said hello to strangers on the street. "We'll get through this," he says, pulling her into him. God, where are the scriptwriters now? he wonders. "I'm here for you. I mean, we have a history, right? We've got this place, our future. That's worth a lot."

"It's your place, mostly," she says, but she's nodding, too. Her nose drips onto his shoulder.

"Maybe what we need is a holiday. I could get the time off."

"We don't have the money for that," she says, truthfully. She drags her hand beneath her nose, sniffs.

"So we do it on VISA. Live now, pay later." He's animated, acting out the commercial. He hopes he's cheering her, because this is not who he is at all. He hates debt, thinks paying off credit cards is like buying a dead horse. "Come on. Greece, New Zealand . . . I hear Russia's a hoot. Or we could walk across England, sleep in castles and get falling down drunk in those little pubs. It'd be like *Coronation Street*. Come on. You know you want to. We could do New York." *And when we're miles away, and the moon's sinking, and you're thinking that this is it, this is as good as it gets, I'll slide in my big news: you'll never have babies with this cowboy.*

"I do love you," she says, squeezing him hard. "Thanks." She kisses him. "I'll get a job — even a shit job, if I have to. Hell, I'll even go back to SaskEnergy. I'm going to work hard, save money. Afterall — " she finds his eyes, " — I've got a wedding to pay for."

He's sinking. The ground's sucking him up like Tarzan in quicksand; the Saturday morning cartoons of his youth. "That's great, Baby. I love you, too."

Another squeeze, then she steps up to the fence where the paint's peeled the worst, begins scratching with the wire brush. The sound is Cajun. "I kind of already told Mom," she confesses. The flecks fly.

"Already?" Down boy. He whips the paint. "Did you tell her *when* we're gracing the altar?"

Eden works her way down the board. "Of course not! You know I'd talk to you first."

I don't know anything anymore, Sam thinks. Except this paint brush is too stiff to do anything with, we should have tied the rose bush back before we began, and I'm in deep, deep shit here.

They work for an hour, finishing the gate and half the fence. Then Eden goes inside to make sandwiches and Sam inspects his bearded irises.

"Ta-da." Eden returns with a pyramid of egg salad sandwiches on a silver tray and grapes for dessert. They devour everything.

"Geez Louise that was good." Sam is tiptoeing, still that other person, that imposter. She loves him, and what he feels for her is as close to love as anything he's ever felt. Muted. Comfortable. Love left out in the rain.

"Let's get back at it."

Eden scrapes, he paints. Then they switch. She's a sloppy painter, her arms, face and hair are spattered with white stars. His flannel shirt's a write-off. She tunes the radio to a Top 40 station and cranks the volume. A dragonfly zings past. Nature — the melodies he yearns for — can't compete. There's the station's call letters, a splitter, the one o'clock news. A young girl has been killed while delivering papers. Her name, the reporter says, was Maria.

❧❧❧

Eden is at the power company, seeing where she can slide back in. Sam calls in sick, says he was lifting gyproc and pulled a muscle in his back, which isn't a stretch: a month ago, while helping his brother drywall a house, he had, in fact, felt a twinge.

He gleaned the funeral information through the newspaper. Maria was in the area when she died; she'd had his paper in her wagon. Sam envisions one small wagon wheel wobbling toward the curb. Then: stillness. It seems an elderly driver suffered a stroke and slammed into the girl as she was crossing the street. Why didn't we hear the sirens? Sam wonders. At what moment did her heart stop? When he was scrubbing paint off his hands, making dispassionate love to Eden, sitting on the toilet reading about hardy perennials? He'd been wrong about her age. She was fourteen, a grade eight student. The obituary named her parents, three siblings, a grandmother. She was fond of animals and liked to ride her bike.

He had read the obituary five times, then clipped it and hid it in the top kitchen shelf, behind the good wine glasses. Senseless. Why that moment? Why could the car not have veered a few feet further down the street? Could he have helped, maybe saved her life? He had First Aid and CPR training. He should have spoken to her. He could have at least said hello.

His black dress pants need pressing. He slides the iron down their length. The material sticks, and his pants shine up at him. He finds his good shirt and the red tie exactly as he left them after a wedding last June. Eden had said he looked like a waiter in a restaurant where they cover the menus in plastic.

The funeral home is a walk away, but he would be too conspicuous for the morning in his creased pants — warm on his thighs — and tie. He gets into his seldom-used Mazda, sees there is a quarter tank of gas, and drives.

His seat is near the back; the room is two-thirds full. He looks at the backs of strangers' heads: bad perms; skater cuts; shaved heads; brunette hair falling from a clip. The crowd is predominantly young, and inappropriately dressed.

Suits in the room clothe men they were not intended for, in colours no longer fashionable. Sams sees feet pinched into shoes that have only ever known runners, cowboy boots, the steel toes of construction. Blue jeans predominate. Toddlers squirm, pinch, and make too much noise.

There are the sounds of grief: tissue and tears and a mournful organ piece piped through hidden speakers. There should be more flowers, Sam thinks. I should have sent daisies or something yellow, something a girl would like.

Two men enter, walking very closely together. Sam realizes they're handcuffed. "Uncle!" a little boy cries. The prisoner waves with his free hand, a self-made tattoo inked into his thumb's web. The guard has a walkie-talkie strapped to his hip. Sam remembers playing walkie-talkies with his brother, seeing how far they could separate and still make out each other's scratchy, "Are you there?"

A woman in a green plaid suit slips in beside Sam, handkerchief pressed to her nose. "It's so awful," she whispers, leaning toward him. "I taught her two years ago."

Sam fingers the program. Maria Rascher. There's an angel embossed on the cover, Maria's school photo inside. She might have had moments of happiness, he thinks. "Very sad."

"Are you family?" the teacher asks, her perfume a strong musk he has to breathe.

"I'm her uncle," Sam says, and the service begins.

জওজ

His hands are buried to the wrists in mud. It's mid-June, almost too late to be planting, but there are holes. Last year his Russian giant sunflowers towered over the garden. In the fall, with their large fringed heads facing the ground, he thought they looked like tall, shy girls who never got asked to dance. The neighbour before Adrienne, an eighty-nine-year-old man of the land, said he used to plant fields of sunflowers and he'd never seen the likes of what Sam had growing right there, smack dab in the middle of the city. Only two sunflowers have reseeded themselves. He scatters seeds among the beginnings of brown-eyed Susans, Chinese lanterns, California and Iceland poppies, lupines.

"What in the world are you doing?" Eden calls from the back step. "It's raining."

He hadn't noticed. There's a dance of drops on the pond, flashes of orange beneath. She'll never dance, he thinks. Maria will never dance. His fish are happy. They are alive. And procreating. "I'm coming in."

He slips off his gardening shoes and carries them in, back slightly stooped after the hours in the garden.

He's becoming an old man, Eden thinks, as he passes her. The phone rings.

She cups the mouthpiece and stage whispers to Sam: "It's Adrienne. She wants us to come for dinner. I won't be able to stay long — I've got that thing with the girls tonight." Eden waits for a reaction. "Well?"

He nods, then drags his feet into the living room, sweeps the room with his eyes. Nothing's moved, and this disappoints him. He's come to expect change to happen of its own volition, as if the rocker would work its way over to the window, the CDs would hop off their shelves. She should not have died, he thinks. Not fair, not fair, not fair.

There's a fungus growing inside his heart.

His feet lead him to the verandah. Now the rain is falling in sheets, blurring the street beyond his windows. Three neighbourhood kids splash barefoot. Sam recognizes Whelan's daughter, a six-year-old with one front tooth.

"Adrienne wants us there at seven." Eden's hair is longer now, and dyed a shade before black. She says she wants it long for the wedding. The ends brush her shoulders; she thinks the style makes her look Egyptian. She's also doing something new with her eyes, but Sam hasn't noticed. "Sam? Is that okay?"

"Yeah, sure." He pulls away from the wet children, crosses the hardwood floor. "I'm going upstairs to work. Call me when it's time to go."

His work is in the room which has been, alternately, a sewing room, an office, a reading room, a storage room, a room with a bed in which no one ever slept. Now it is something else. Sam grabs the flathead screwdriver on the window ledge and unscrews the switchplate. He does the same with all the electrical outlet covers. The mini blinds are stuck into their moors. He wedges the screwdriver in and they reluctantly snap out. Masking tape is applied around windows, doorframes and above the narrow baseboards. Next he cracks open the paint, swirls a paint stick around the cotton candy colour. Eden had frowned at his choice: "Pink? Who paints a guest room pink?"

He dips the brush in, steps onto his footstool and slathers colour down the wall. Soon it's blushing back at him. He hums.

"Sam," Eden is calling. "It's time."

He props the windows open. "Bye for now," he whispers to the ghosts beneath the walls. The door clicks shut behind him.

જાજાજા

Adrienne's house smells like salmon. "You can take the girl off the coast, but you can't take the coast out of the girl."

The three of them eat a quiet dinner. The women discuss recent movies, the relative calm since the drug dealer has been evicted. Sam says almost nothing.

"I'm sorry I have to run," Eden apologizes. "I already had plans." She rises to start clearing the table.

Adrienne touches Eden's wrist. "Don't worry about this. I'll take care of it."

Eden thanks her again, kisses Sam's cheek, and leaves. Adrienne piles the dishes.

"I'll help," Sam says, lifting the salmon plate away.

"You sure? I don't have a dishwasher, you know."

Sam grabs a dishtowel off the stove. There's an African violet on the windowsill above the sink. A spider plant spills out of its pot above the fridge. Splashes of green beg his attention in every corner of the room. He fingers a book on prairie gardening as Adrienne fills the sink. The words blur; a language he's forgotten.

Adrienne nudges him with her elbow. "So, how are you? I haven't talked to you for so long, I was beginning to think you were mad at me."

"What? Oh man, I'm sorry. I've been busy." His face feels very warm. "I'm working on a project in the house."

"No kidding." She runs a glass under water, sets it on the drying tray. "What project?"

"A room we've never really done anything with. Our spare room. I'm painting it, putting in a new rug."

"So that's why I haven't seen you outside." She passes a handful of dripping cutlery. Their wet hands graze. Now she's staring out the window at the fence between their yards. Earlier she'd hacked out the creeping Charlie that had crawled over from his side. The plants next door are strangling each other: weeds, gangly brown-eyed Susans, anorexic sunflowers. She adds more water to the sink. "Can I come see it some time?"

"The room? Sure. Whenever."

"Good. I will." She drags her cloth over a dish. "Sam, is there something you've been keeping a secret?"

He wears a question on his face.

"So it's not a nursery?"

"A nursery? No." If he could remember how to laugh, he would do it now.

ʖʖʖ

Eden opens the door slowly, like a trespasser, though what has been happening here is no secret to her. The paint smell is long gone but the scent of newness remains. There's a border, midway up the wall: dancing ballerinas. New bed and white headboard, white dresser, a bookshelf. The bed is covered in a pink floral comforter, with a solid pink bedskirt and matching shams. She runs her hand down the length of the pretty bed. On the bookshelf he's paired a white teddy bear with a black-haired doll. A porcelain carousel, when wound, spins out "Für Elise." A nameplate on the dresser spells "Maria."

It has taken him months to create. Nights, weekends, his holidays. September disappeared and October is escaping. There is, for him, only work now, and this pink, daughterless room. Eden sees it for what it is: his New York. She knew the medical truth even before he did, had her IUD yanked in January. But what of this? What to do with this? She hears him unlocking the front door, his footsteps across the floor. She meets him in the stairwell. "You're early," she says. "I haven't even begun to think about dinner. Hungry?"

"No."

She didn't expect any other answer. He looks gaunt, anemic; she's been trying to get him to the doctor.

"Don't go," he says, and she holds his bones like a protective sister.

જીજીજી

Paris.

Eden is sitting in an outdoor café eating a baguette. It is morning, and she is not alone. Something about the quality of light, the air's snap, pink tulips on every table; a vessel of memory bursts. "I knew a man once," she begins, "this was years ago. He knew the Latin names of any plant you could think of."

Her companion leans forward and rests his chin on his hands, folded, as if in prayer.

"Nothing delighted him more than to walk through his small garden on a morning — say a morning like this — to see how everything was progressing. There was a pond, and goldfish. They came to know him."

"How do you know?"

"They'd swim to kiss his fingertips when he stirred the water. It made him happy."

"They only came when he did it?"

"Yes. It made him happy," she repeats. "It was enough."

The waiter arrives. *"Désirez-vous reprende du café?"*

"Merci, non," her companion says. "You loved this man?"

"He had passions."

"That's not what I asked."

She waits a long moment. "He has a place in my heart, yes. I loved him. We almost married."

"Almost?"

"Like I said, he had passions."

"Ah . . . another woman."

"You might say."

The waiter returns with their bill. At the next table young lovers get up together and a glass is upset. There are quick words, a flurry of white napkins — not much, but enough to take Eden away, and then it is almost entirely gone: a lifetime, a moment, eight years — what time has tumbled so completely into the past the relationship might have been the territory of dreams or the eclipse of a stranger's conversation, but the colour around it — yes, she's smelling it now — the apple green colour remains.

WHEN THE CAR COMES SHE FREES THE ELASTIC FROM HER HAIR, creates a curtain for her swollen, tear-stung face. God, she thinks, I must look like hell.

"*Perdón*. Excuse me, can I help you?"

He turns on an interior light. She sees a wide, tanned face with high, good bones, eyes the same blue as her own, curly hair cut short, wraparound sunglasses pushed onto his crown. Not Venezuelan. Twenty-six? she wonders. Thirty-three? Mud is caked over the wheel wells of his Honda Prelude.

"*¿Hablas inglés?* Are you okay?" he asks.

"I don't know. I've lost my ATM card. I'm — " She points over her shoulder at the bank machine that swallowed it. "I guess I'm stranded."

He opens his door, takes a few steps toward her. Good shorts — khaki, with a crease — and a white tank top. He's dressed much better than I am, she notes. Looks genuinely concerned. Not someone whose *cojones* I'll likely be kicking in, she decides.

"I've lost my automated teller card," she repeats, "in that machine. I don't know what to do. My money was stolen, my hotel is — "

He takes a cigarette from his shirt pocket. "I'm Cory, Cory Schaan."

He offers his hand.

"Mallard," she says, "from Canada."

"Which part?"

"Winnipeg."

"Don't know Winnipeg," he says, "just Vancouver, Calgary, Toronto and Montreal. Oh, and I once got a misdirected e-mail from a guy in Turtleford, Saskatchewan." He stretches the final *a* — an American, she thinks — then he smiles, revealing large, neatly aligned teeth. "I'm from Portland, but I have business here."

She wipes her face with her beach towel and begins fidgeting her hair into a single braid. "What kind of business?"

"Condos. The company I work for buys old buildings all over South America and fixes them up. Mostly we finish what other contractors abandon when they run out of money. We sell to a lot of retired dentists in Oregon."

"Oh. Sounds like a great job." She is starting to feel almost normal, thinks this would be a pleasant conversation if she weren't broke, hungry and slumped on a dusty curb in the middle of a South American city with her ATM card jammed in a machine.

"Come on, why don't I give you a lift back to your hotel? Do you want to call your friends . . . tell them you're on your way?" He clicks a cellphone off his belt.

Tricky, she thinks. Should she trust this person who has shown compassion, speaks English, and knows there's a Turtleford, Saskatchewan? Should she lie?

An hour ago she could have killed someone with her rage, but now . . . "I'm travelling alone."

"Okay, well, I guess I'll just drop you off then."

He ducks inside the car and unlocks but doesn't open the passenger door for her. She stands beside it a moment, fingers on the handle, notes the little silver dings around the lock, as if someone with particularly bad aim — a drunk or a small child — had tried to unlock the door and kept missing. Someone like Andrew.

"Where to?"

"The Regal Inn. It's by — "

"The Hilton. I know. Properties are my business."

A trifle pretentious, she thinks, but he *is* giving her a ride, and that is kind. There are kind people everywhere you go, she's learned. Lots of assholes, too. Her own brother, Grant, a thirty-year-old former Western Hockey League hero who drives a milk truck in Brandon, fits that category. He had never been supportive of her marriage to a man who didn't follow organized sports, didn't even have a favourite NHL team. But that was among Andrew's charms.

"Mallard. Funky name." Cory starts a smile but doesn't carry through. "Your parents named you after a duck."

"My father's idea. He's a wildlife biologist, retired now. When I was fourteen I switched the d to y and became Mallary." The dashboard is luminous, the interior neat; definitely one of the better cars on the island, she imagines.

Cory glances at her. "So why'd you introduce yourself as Mallard?"

She is feeling much better now. She's having a sane conversation with someone other than herself. The mess with the jammed bank card and her missing ID can be sorted out tomorrow. Things could be worse. She isn't hurt. She isn't dying. "An alias. Just in case."

They pass a battered Ford half-ton with a rope wrapped around the hood, presumably to keep it from flying into the windshield. In the box, five Venezuelans sway and stumble against one another. They are drinking beer, looking happy.

"Would you like to stop for something to eat before I drop you off? There's a pretty good restaurant at the —"

"No thanks. It's nice of you to offer but you're already doing me a huge favour with this ride. I don't want you to spend any money on me."

He clucks his tongue against the roof of his mouth. "What if I cooked? Did I tell you that I was a chef in a former life? I just bought groceries. How about a good old-fashioned steak and potatoes meal?" He glances at her again. She hesitates. "Come on, you must be getting a little sick of — let me guess — pizza and chicken?"

She can't help herself; she laughs. "Actually, I've been living on soup and bread mostly. Trying to cut costs and all that."

"I hear ya, but — " He checks something in his rearview mirror. Mallary turns: two young Venezuelan women in short, wrap-around skirts and bikini tops are crossing the street behind them. She thinks about saying something — "Friends of yours?" — but stops herself. Her corner should be coming up after the next major intersection, right by the billboard with the graffiti: *FUCHO*, Humberto *y* Juan, and the crude, adolescent drawings of genitalia that she has seen spray painted on billboards, fences, buildings and bridges in every city she's ever travelled to.

"So, are we on? Will you eat with me?"

It would be a slightly radical thing to do, she thinks. It's enough that she is here alone, enough that she has accepted a ride from a stranger. She's really not the type to —

"Nice salad, some rolls . . . mouth watering yet?"

It is. "Okay, but I've got to make a call. I'll reverse the charges."

"No sweat, you wanna use this?" He holds up the cellphone.

She evaluates his hand. Small for a man, she thinks, with square nails, all the half-moons of his cuticles clearly visible. His nails are in better shape than mine, except, perhaps, for one. "I think I'll wait."

❧❧❧

By the sea. The translation alone had been enough to tempt her to Porlamar, a tourist city — duty free and sun guaranteed — on the eastern edge of Isla de Margarita. She had been too tired to explore on her first day. There were delays at Pearson — ice on the wings — and remarkable chaos at the island airport, but the second morning she discovered two routes to the nearest beach: one via the neighbouring Hilton, where she felt like a trespasser wandering through the cool, tile-glazed lobby to the maze of pools, then past a thin fringe of palms to the beach; the other through a condominium construction site.

Condos were plugging up the coastline: white, overpriced, multi-storey boxes with huge *VENDER o ALQUILAR* banners draped across the balconies. Miles of wire wrapped in corrugated metal whipped out of the dirt like pythons ready to strike. A squat, barefoot man carrying two boards over his shoulder had watched her pick her way over the debris of concrete and lumber. Above her, from a precarious scaffolding of stripped and banged-together trees, another Venezuelan whistled. He megaphoned his hands, called: *"¡Guapa!"* Pretty.

Playa Moreno. A long, unremarkable beach littered with broken glass, dead pufferfish, pebbles licked smooth by waves, gnarled fingers of seaweed and what Mallary sincerely hoped was only dog shit. There had been no one in the water so she did not chance it herself, although the heat was a wet towel she wore like a bodybag.

First that, then, today, she had found herself standing before a ghostly fair — warm wind sighed through the skeleton of an idle Ferris wheel and a roller coaster that had not inspired a scream in months. Another attraction listed in Andrew's travel books — another on the long list of disappointments she'd encountered since arriving eight days earlier.

She had walked in every direction, trying to get her bearings in the city, so much smaller than her own but so much harder to draft into a comprehensible mental map. A taxi slid up along the curb, cardboard license plate dangling from a wire, the driver's face obscured by a web of windshield cracks. *"¿Taxi?"*

"No *gracias*." Mallary held his gaze long enough to measure politeness. There was an art to everything here, rejection included. The islanders would not let her be just a woman, walking. *"Prefiero caminar."*

"¿Es usted de Argentina?"

She considered his mistake a compliment. Must be the tan, she imagined, or the few Spanish phrases she wrapped her tongue around, thanks to conversation classes. "No, *Canadiense*."

"Bueno." His car threw up the fine white dust that had settled over the afternoon like snow.

She hadn't known what to do with herself. The sea was east, the town, Pampatar, and the 17th-century Castillo de San Carlos de Borromeo, which she had already toured, north. There were good beaches nearby, but she had visited each of them already, and had burned her face so badly she lost a band of skin above her eyes. She hid the damage beneath a ball cap, her blonde-streaked ponytail slipped through the back. South would take her along the shops, restaurants and hotels on Avenida Bolivar, the route that lead to *El Centro* — the heart and headquarters of all of the city's juxtapositions. The designer shops on Avenida Quatro de Mayo were breaths away from the *barrios* where lost men and toothless grandmothers sat in doorways and chickens freewheeled in front yard dirt. There *turistas* who did not know any better — or were just plain lost in their rented cars — had pearls scratched right off their necks. Mallary had seen the ugly marks.

She squinted west. Jungle mountains were half buried in the mist that wrapped them each day like a woolly scarf, threatening but rarely delivering rain. She wanted to hike into the jungle, find brown capuchin monkeys free of ankle chains, unlike the sad, inhibited little fellows she had seen at a bar on Playa Caribe. But how could she do that? How does one walk right into the jungle? It appeared close, but each time she thought she was nearing it, it retreated, like a mirage.

Soon the dark — a sudden splash of ink across the sky — and she hadn't eaten since breakfast: her hotel's eternal offering of croissants, mixed fruit and toast proved too much of a good thing. She washed the fare down with tea, but the waiters made even that difficult. They could not get it right, brought water with milk in it and a tea bag on the side; cold milk with a tea bag floating on the surface like an air mattress in a miniature pool. Andrew would have thought this funny. Andrew, the real Andrew, not the one people saw in the frail husk he had become, still would.

She was starting to miss home.

She crossed the road and entered a serene residential area. No chickens. No salsa blasting from windows. No bone-racked dogs oozing pus from wounds incurred in traffic; nothing hopping after her on three legs. The *casas* affected affluence: whitewashed homes, red corrugated roofs, barred windows and seven-foot concrete fences studded with shards of glass. The perfume of hibiscus made her spin. Who lived here?

The hour had become increasingly surreal. There should be people around, she thought — a child chasing a ball onto the street, women with shopping in their arms — but there was only a stillness that amplified the grinding of microscopic pebbles beneath her shoes. What would Andrew have made of this? she wondered. Before he got sick, when they'd first married, he would have filled the silence with words. He had, at times, been uncomfortable without noise colouring the white holes of space and time.

Several minutes passed before she discovered the shopping centre. She darted across the road, backpack and the water bottle inside clunking against her spine. Inside the mall she languidly perused grocery aisles. Should she buy for two days, or three?

There was a commotion at the meat counter: someone had stepped ahead of someone else. How was that possible? There were only three men in line and each had a numbered ticket, just like at the passport office. She studied the sign on the display case. Some familiar words — *queso, jamón, tocino, pollo* — but most were totally outside the borders of her memorized nouns and verbs in present tense.

She cruised each aisle, selected shampoo, a can of vegetable soup, three apples, a small jar of peanut butter, then stood in line to pay. The backpack slid down her arm. The clerk — an effeminate man with crusts of eczema between his fingers — began punching in prices.

Her wallet was gone. She opened the pack's main pouch, yanked out her towel and water bottle. "Oh no."

The clerk waited.

She swept the bottom of her pack, but only sand turned up on her fingertips. Money, passport, VISA. Every fucking thing gone. *"Lo siento. No puedo encontrar mi dinero."*

The clerk scowled. His fingers were cupped over the cash register like an organist playing chords. He pulled a straw out of his shirt pocket, pinched the end and stuck it between his teeth. He looks bored, Mallary thought, as if this kind of thing happened every hour. She jabbed her fingers into the pockets of her cut-offs. Her room key was there, in the front, and — thank God! — she'd stuck her bank card in a back pocket.

"¿Aceptan esta tarjeta?" Most stores did now, at least in Canada.

"No lo aceptan. El banco está a tres manzanas de aquí." He pointed at the north wall with the straw. *"Hay una* ATM." Three blocks, presumably north.

Someone had stolen her wallet, likely when she'd been in the water at Playa el Agua.

She left her groceries and bolted toward the exit. She needed to eat. She stopped two boys doing figure-eights on their bikes. *"¿Dondé está el banco, por favor?"*

The boy in a red T-shirt leaned through his handlebars. "Huh?"

"¿Dondé está—"

"Follow me." The other boy, an attractive blond with skin like iced cappuccino, wheeled his bike around.

"No puedo — I-I can't pay you. I've lost all my money." She pulled the pockets out of her shorts to show them. *"No tengo nada."*

The pretty boy looked at his friend, then at her. Had she insulted him? Perhaps his father is a doctor, or a prominent businessman. Maybe the boy was the son of an important politician, how could she know? Shit. It was a stupid mistake to make, and she hoped they would not reject her for it.

"No hay problema, chica. Sigueme."

She jogged behind the boys so they did not have to walk their bikes. The sky was pressing down, a velvety black, the air turning cool. The boys swung left at the end of the parking lot, passed cinderblock buildings with bars on the windows, weaved through a park where garbage spilled across the grass. Mallary scratched the zigzag route into her arm with her one sharp fingernail. Ever since she was twelve and the teachers at Glenelm School sent the students home with notes about a pervert offering children candy, she had kept the nail on her right pointer finger long and sharp. She glazed it with clear polish to keep it strong.

The bank was on the corner. *"Muchas gracias."*

"De nada." The boys spun away.

She inserted her ATM card, punched the code. Nothing. She pushed the button to end the transaction. A beep, but her card did not pop out. She repeated the process. Not even a beep. She pounded the machine, stabbed more buttons. Nothing.

I want my mother. The first thing that came to her, though her mother had been dead five years. She had felt this most basic need — to be comforted in the arms of her mother — at two other times in her adult life: when she'd had a violent flu that compelled her to shuck blankets one moment, scramble beneath them the next, and the morning Andrew's doctor spelled the letters ALS. Amyotrophic lateral sclerosis. That scene could have been scripted, it was so movie-like. "It's Lou Gehrig's," Andrew had said. "I'm doomed."

❧❧❧

It is an elaborate condo, with pine furniture, lots of plants and dramatic area rugs in geometric designs. Straight out of an IKEA catalogue, she muses.

"It's the show suite," Cory says. "Have a look around."

"Thanks, I will, but I'd like to call my dad first. Where's the — " She spies the phone in the galley kitchen.

"There's one in there, too, if you want." He hands her a flute of red wine and points down the hall. "My room."

Privacy. "Thanks."

Her muffled footfalls on the carpeted hallway remind her that her feet have not touched a rug since her changeover hotel in Toronto. "Isn't it a little impractical to have carpets in here," she calls, "being so close to the beach, I . . . mean? Especially light colours like this?"

She can hear him opening cupboard doors. "We've got maids. It's not a problem."

"*Nada* problem," she says beneath her breath.

The operator understands her, first try, and soon she is listening to the ring heard in her father's kitchen, thousands of miles away. *Pick up, Dad!* After the fourth ring the answering machine clicks on and she quickly explains her predicament. "But I'm okay! Really... I'm fine. Say hello to Andrew for me." She hopes her father has been visiting regularly. Andrew knows, she assures herself. He knows.

When she returns to the kitchen, Cory is tearing a head of lettuce apart; a chore he appears comfortable with. She believes him, about being a chef, but she's still considering the wider person. Maybe she's committed herself to a meal with the biggest jerk on the island. He could be anyone.

"Have a seat, turn on the TV. Changer should be on the couch." Cory sets the lettuce down and puts the fingertips of both hands on her shoulders, steering her out of the galley. "You sit, I cook. There's more wine."

She refills her glass, careful not to spill. She clicks through four channels, but nothing interests her as much as the view from the balcony. She's surprised to recognize the rocky crags about a half mile offshore. Playa Moreno, the far south end.

Her host slides past with steaks, then forks them onto the barbecue. "Medium rare okay?"

"Lovely." The wine, she thinks, might be giving her a buzz, but more than anything she is wiped out, could sleep through the rest of her vacation and be deliriously happy to do it. Twenty-seven years old and she feels like sixty, her father's age. It has all been too much: Andrew, disappearing one sad piece at a time before they had even celebrated their third anniversary; then her friends and father supporting this trip as a mental health break, though the latter had wished she had not insisted on travelling alone. "Sometimes you've got less sense than a dog."

She had been helpless bystander the first year, nursemaid for the next two, and now that Andrew was in a hospice, she was the young wife grieving, not death, but his shattered life — *their* shattered lives.

"It's ready." Cory calls her to the pine dining room table. They eat, and it is as if she is making up for all those soup and bread meals of the last eight days.

After, she can hardly move, even pulls her top out of her shorts, then surreptitiously slips her fingers underneath to undo the button. "That was excellent."

"Thanks. It wasn't anything fancy. Let's just leave these." He pushes his plate forward, but returns the ice water to the fridge. Mallary follows with her eyes as he leaves the kitchen and plops onto the couch with all the pillows, in the adjoining room. He slides a video out of the entertainment centre. "You coming over?" He cracks the case, slides the video out.

Should she ask for a ride home now? Eat and run? She is, she reminds herself, still at his mercy. "Sure."

She takes a chair across from him, crossing her legs beneath her, making it seem like an assured, casual choice to sit as far away as possible and still be in the same room. "Whatcha watching?"

He is fastforwarding through opening credits. "I don't know what it is. The other guy who stays here — we alternate — he must have left it."

The film opens with an overhead shot of a large campus: old, grey buildings, attractive students walking in twos and threes, books clutched to their chests or tucked beneath arms. It's summer. Hairstyles and clothes are retro, which means it could either have been shot last month or twenty-five years ago. As soon as the dialogue begins and the camera closes in on a young female professor's *chichis* — the movie's in Spanish — Mallary knows it doesn't matter when it was made.

She sits up and stretches to gaze out the patio door. Through the concrete slats in the balcony she sees a blink of light on the ocean. A cruise ship, maybe. Very far away. She imagines people dancing on the deck, an orchestra with musicians in suits so white they hurt the eye, trombones and trumpets gleaming. She sees old men playing shuffleboard, lovers finding a rhythm on gently rocking beds.

After she and Andrew had found out about the Lou Gehrig's, sex didn't matter much anymore. It was something other people did, people who didn't have to worry about the degeneration of nerves and muscles, about how that translated into not being able to lift an arm to touch someone's cheek, shake a hand, button a shirt. Sex was for people who had no worries about wheelchairs and powers of attorney. She would sacrifice anything just to hear Andrew say her name again, to see him walk across the room into her arms, like a toddler learning first steps.

She turns back to the screen. The classroom has emptied and the *profesora* is alone now, wiping chalk notes off the board. A door opens and a pockmarked man with a long ponytail — a colleague? a student? — presses against her, pinning her right hand against the board. With his free hand he undoes her skirt and slides it over her hips, revealing pear-shaped buttocks and a small, star-shaped tattoo.

Mallary sneaks a look at Cory. His knees are up, feet bare against the edge of the glass coffee table. She notes flushed cheeks, his right hand moving in the pocket of his shorts. Oh, God. So that's what's going on, she thinks. Does he know I know? She tests her one long fingernail against her thumb. Tonight, finally, she might have to use it.

They're on the desk now. The man's opened her white blouse and is squeezing her left breast while his tongue traces her right nipple. *"¡Sí sí sí!"* There is other dialogue, but Mallary didn't learn those kinds of words in her Spanish class.

The ponytailed man peels off the slash of material — hardly enough there to call them panties — that covers the *profesora*'s genitals.

The television, at medium volume, is not enough to mask Cory's breathy sounds. Mallary moves her head a fraction of an inch. He has it out, in his right palm, thumb kneading the top third, near the tip. Liar. He knew exactly which movie this was, she realizes. The bastard wanted an audience.

The actors roll into the 69 position and she looks away as the camera closes in. She's never seen anything as hardcore as this. Or maybe this isn't even considered hardcore; what does she know about smut?

No one would believe this. She wishes there were someone to share it with, but she does not see it ever coming out. She can't tell Andrew. Her brother: never. Maybe a close friend in some far away, future moment, when she's thirty-five and their children are laughing and soaking themselves in the lawn sprinkler a safe distance away.

No. She is already doing it. She is already marrying herself to someone who is not Andrew, someone who will not die before her eyes. Andrew was supposed to be here. He'd bought those damn books, enrolled them in Spanish classes, promised they would see as much of the world as possible.

It's the smack of all-out screwing now. Cory moans, the sound a hum against his lips, then again, louder. He's jerking off with both hands now: one makes a dice shuffling motion, the other a flat-palmed circling across the head.

"Uh-uh-uh." He doesn't seem to care how much noise he's making. Then:

"Ooooh."

The actors are not finished yet, but Cory picks up the channel changer and clicks the film off. He skirts around the back of the couch and disappears into the washroom, closing the door with a click. Why the modesty now? Mallary wonders.

She is fixed on a light out at sea — a cruise ship — where she must believe that someone is hurting no one.

"I'll take you to your hotel now."

When she gets out of the car, it's him, not her, saying thank you.

↪↪↪

Mallary's last evening on the island.

Her father called an hour ago: Andrew has been slipping further into the abyss — it is a good thing she is going home. She sits at the hotel bar; Ernesto is mixing a long pink drink. They're both watching a Latin dance channel on the miniature television suspended from the ceiling; for Mallary it's just a place to look.

"*Recuérdame*," Ernesto says, handing her the drink along with a white paper flower, a napkin folded into a rose. Remember me. Inside the petals, he has written his phone number.

"*Claro*," she says. Of course. She writes her phone number on another napkin, changing the last two numbers. The drink slides down her throat and in three minutes is gone. She pays Ernesto, leaving a generous tip. After tomorrow she'll have no use for *bolivares*.

She pushes through the Regal Inn's glass doors, breathes the raw and tossing sea. *Perfecto*. Another exemplary night in paradise. There's a show at the Hilton tonight — one of those audience participation events; unamusing to everyone except the intoxicated and easily entertained. Not for her. She sits on the step, stretches her arms out behind her, leans back and closes her eyes, listening, with each of her immaculate cells, for the music of cruise ships, the orchestra of the long lost steps.

WHAT DO YOU THINK YOUR LIFE MEANS?

THE COW WAS ABSOLUTELY, POSITIVELY, ONE HUNDRED PERCENT dead. The awful sounds had stopped and it hadn't tried to lift its massive head for at least ten minutes now. If all Lovilla could see were the head alone, she might think it was just sleeping there in the middle of the highway, but further along, slightly above the point where the stiff front legs joined the body, swamps of dark blood had oozed through the mangy white hide, and below that — God, she hated to look — the side was smashed in and there were broken bones poking every which way. A coil of pink intestine made her stomach roll and there was something blue and soft, like a clump of porridge. A hind leg was bent at an unlikely angle, as if the cow were doing the can-can, but backwards.

It was four-thirty in the afternoon, the temperature neither warm nor cool. She'd been standing beside the dead cow for approximately twenty minutes and no cars had come. Roger had said he'd be right back. She had wanted to go with him, but he'd said that she should stay there, beside the cow, in case a car came and didn't see it and then they might be responsible for a lot more than the loss of one unlucky Hereford. Well, she could see the wisdom in that, so she stepped out in her new suit with the almost matching shoes and wrapped her long jacket over her arm, like a butler in the movies, then waved her husband away with *Hurry* hooked in her throat.

"Back as soon as possible!" Roger had said, his voice echoing back from the wall of trees beyond the ditch. "We've still got plenty of time to make the meeting." She watched as he ducked his slightly radish-shaped head — his sisters still called him "Radish" when they were in a teasing mood; the nickname he'd been trying to shake since grade four — to get into the car. The front end was crunched and they'd lost a headlight but the car was driveable.

Lovilla tapped along the shoulder of the highway to the top of a rise and looked south, the direction they'd come from. They were in a rolling, forested section of country, a surprise after one hundred and fifty miles of knee-high canola and barley crops, and another field that Roger guessed was echinacea, the wonder drug for the common cold. His older sister was married to a farmer but Roger had only a rudimentary knowledge of all things agricultural, gleaned from his occasional perusal of the *Western Producer*. Any crop he didn't recognize he guessed was echinacea.

Before they'd entered the Northern Provincial Forest they'd been playing a game: rating each farm they passed on a scale of one to five. They considered the houses, the barns and outbuildings, the number of granaries, the shape the fences were in, the order of the yards and gardens, whether a large, stupid dog ran out to the highway and barked after them, or not. They had been discussing the virtues of the last farm when the collision occurred. Roger had only given the farm a three, but Lovilla had liked the fact that there were clean sheets snapping on the clothesline, and a treehouse for the children — the real kids, and her own, imagined babies — to tell secrets in. They'd start trying soon, Roger had said. If things panned out up here, they'd get at it directly.

"It was at least a four," she'd argued. "Did you see how well the potatoes were doing? And the grass was all cut in that crisscross method. It was almost perfect."

Roger looked at her and snorted. "Perfect! What about that beat-up swather in the ditch? Ten to one it's out of commission. And who wants to farm anyway? Prices have gone to hell, you're at the mercy of the weather, chemical companies, grasshoppers, and — "

"It's just a game, Roger." God, sometimes. She flipped the subject. "I don't want to move. I checked the phone book. The town only has ten pages."

"Please, don't start with that again." He groaned, as he was apt to whenever she brought up the subject of staying in the city. The sound was like a piano being pushed across hardwood. Lovilla thought of gouges.

Roger continued. "You know this is a great opportunity for me. A golden opportunity. I could be vice-principal in a few years, if things go okay. And you yourself said it'd be good to get away, after what happened."

"Yeah." She looked at the trees. What had happened was a bank robbery, a man in a Texaco toque sticking a gun in her ear while everyone else — the other tellers, the loans officer, Mrs. Herb Sawatsky and Mrs. Frank Penner, who'd come in together to cash their pension cheques — dropped to the floor as ordered. Police dogs trapped the guy in an alley two hours later. She was given a three week stress leave, with pay and counselling, although she felt she really didn't need the latter.

Her sister, Ara, a university student, had picked her brains about it. Ara considered herself an authority on psychology, philosophy and religion after first year classes in each. She asked deep, impossible questions. "How did you feel?" she'd asked, leaning on her elbows over a thick mug of mocha in one of the trendy cappuccino bars she loved to frequent. "Do you think it will change you?"

Roger was talking about the farm again. "And I know you. You'd hate to be tied down with chickens and an acre of garden . . . all that canning, taking meals out to the field. Ha! I'm changing my score. Two point five." He was facing her. It had become a challenge.

"You're not allowed to change," Lovilla had argued. "Besides, it's at least a four, maybe even — "Then they'd broadsided the cow and she screamed. She'd screamed when Roger stood over it, slowly shaking his head, and she screamed now, because it was all she could do.

She walked back to the cow, watched it for movement. Nothing. Her feet hurt in the new shoes. Lavender, a shade darker than her suit, with pointed toes and slingback heels, though they were well into August and it was likely too late for slingbacks. She thought of the picture she must make, all gussied up with a dead cow in the middle of — well, wherever the Sam hell she was. Ridiculous. It was surreal — one of Ara's favourite new words. It was like the collage her sister had hanging above her bed — a sailboat, a banana split, JFK's head—none of it making a sniff of sense.

Her throat hurt from the screaming. She heard a rumbling from the south. Roger! The sad but not unreasonably angry farmer would be following in a grain truck, or, more likely, he'd pull up in some large piece of equipment that would scoop the beast off the road. Maybe his wife would be with him. Maybe she was the woman who'd hung the sheets and planted the giant marigolds, loitering like yellow, mop-headed dolls in front of the house they'd most recently passed.

She squinted toward the sound. It was not Roger. She leapt to the middle of the highway, straddled the centre line in front of the cow and began frantically waving before she had time to think.

It was a dusty four-door sedan with a man and two adolescent children inside. The driver pulled his car to a stop about fifteen feet away but seemed hesitant to get out.

She approached his window; he'd rolled it halfway down. "I'm sorry about this, but we've had an accident and hit a cow. You see it there?" She pointed and the family shifted their attention from her to the cow. Of course they saw it.

It was big and dead and oozing God knew what. A chorus of flies was having a picnic in its guts.

The man said nothing.

"My husband's gone to get help. We didn't want anyone else to hit it. If you just drive around . . . "

He was leaning over his window, looking at her shoes, and frowning. The boy in the back — a lumpy kid with his hair shaved around his ears as if he was on leave from the army — asked, "Can we go see?"

The driver snapped his neck around and barked.

She didn't know what else to say, so she stepped away from the car and made a large sweeping motion with her right arm, like a traffic cop, directing them around the obstruction.

"Are you okay?" the man finally asked, hanging out his window.

"Oh yes, quite all right," she answered cheerfully. "My husband will be . . . " but he was passing her now, and she saw that his license plate was sheathed in mud. The boy in the back twisted around so he could see the spectacle from a new angle. She gave a small, queenly wave with a cupped hand, then she cursed Roger and went to sit and sulk in the ditch, with no shoes on. She considered screaming some more, but her throat hurt too much already.

Some time passed before she heard another vehicle, but it was coming from the wrong direction, coming fast, and it was not Roger. She took up her post near the cow and shook her jacket like a matador. The young man behind the wheel of the half-ton hit his brakes and skidded to a stop. "What the hell?" he yelled, leaping from the cab.

"There's been an accident," she said, amazed at how easy the words were becoming, as if they were a greeting — How do you do? Nice day isn't it? — and had nothing to do with the mess on the highway

"No friggin' shit!" He had an orange goatee and red eyes, a ball cap spun backward on his head. Greasy tracks down his faded jeans suggested he'd recently performed an oil change and wiped his hands on his thighs. The sleeves of his black T-shirt looked as though they'd been chewed off. His arms were thin and hairless, and there was an indecipherable word tattooed on his forearm. She could make out an *L*. He kicked the cow's rump. "Dead as a friggin' doornail."

She could feel him looking at her now. Damn you, Roger!

"So, where ya headed?"

"I'm just waiting. My husband will be right back. He's just gone to locate the owner of this cow, and . . . "

"You wanna lift somewhere or something? I got rye and Pepsi in the truck."

She dared to look at him. His eyes were very close together. It was possible that his parents had been related, she thought. He put a handrolled cigarette to his lips, then spit some tobacco off his tongue.

"No thanks. I'll be fine." Goddamn son of a bitch, Roger.

He was still easing his eyes across her. Sizing her up, no doubt. Undressing her. She forced a smile, knowing it was see-through.

"Thanks for stopping, but I don't want to keep you. It's — " she checked her watch " — almost suppertime. I'm sure he'll be here right away."

The boy stood there, smoking. Some of the exhaled smoke looped over his top lip and was sucked back in through his nostrils. Several seconds passed. The only sound was orchestrated by flies, which seemed to be multiplying at an unnatural speed, their buzzing a small roar to Lovilla's ears.

She crossed her arms and stared right into the young man's sore-looking eyes. Was he trying to scare her? She wanted to say: Did you hear about that bank robbery in the city a few weeks back? I'm the teller that was held up. I just emptied out each cash drawer and handed over the money like it was nothing, easy as one, two, three. I survived that, she wanted to tell him, so I sure as hell can survive you. "Really," she said, a vinegar of annoyance seeping into her voice. "You can go. Now."

"Whoa! I was just trying to help. Jesus. Your old man hit this thing on purpose so he could ditch ya?" He stomped toward his truck and she saw that his jeans bagged extravagantly in the seat, as if the cheeks of his ass were inverted. He stopped to pick up a stone and wing it into the trees with one skinny arm. "Screw you!"

He squealed away, much as he'd arrived, and as his truck disappeared over the next hill, she put it together. H-E-L-L. Of course. The ink on his arm spelled HELL.

∾∾∾

Roger had gone into education late. High school math and history: Lovilla couldn't imagine a duller combination. For the last two years he'd been substitute teaching but the truth they'd both finally recognized was that in order to get a full-time position, they were going to have to move. Her salary as a bank teller and his erratic teaching schedule put them in what they euphemistically referred to as a financially challenging situation.

"First impressions are everything," Roger had said, and she'd agreed it was more than a cliché. So she wore new shoes and her new suit, and Roger sported his freshly drycleaned pants. She had wondered about the slingbacks. Were they a fashion *faux pas*? Would the education director's wife see right through her, and Roger, too, with his shiny creases and dress socks that were close — a navy knee-high (hers) on his left foot, which was a full size smaller than his right — but not a true match? His good shoes were a decade old, but men's shoes never really changed much from century to century. They, at least, would do just fine.

Lovilla felt her feet swelling like two loaves of bread inside her shoes. She was exhausted and her neck hurt. Whiplash, she thought. Maybe a concussion. Maybe she wasn't feeling the worst of the pain yet because she was still in shock. Maybe Roger had driven off the road and died from dehydration or blood loss or from having a steering wheel jammed into his spleen. Stupid bloody cow! What was it doing in the middle of the road? She inspected it again. The blood was drying up, the flies were feasting, a hawk was circling overhead. The sight no longer turned her stomach, and really, she decided it wasn't the cow's fault after all. It was Roger's. He never kept his eyes on the damn road. Something like this was destined to happen.

Surely Ara would have lots to offer on today's drama, Lovilla thought. Although five years younger, she considered herself infinitely smarter and more worldly, though the episode with the bank robbery had given her older sister some points. Ara, twenty-three, had asked, "What do you think your life means?"

The sun was sliding behind the trees, leaving the horizon an alabaster pink.

Lovilla was not going to stand beside the cow any longer, waving like a lunatic if anyone came by. She crossed the narrow ditch and took a few tentative steps into the trees, mentally naming them for diversion: black poplar, white poplar, aspen, birch and the almighty, intermittent spruce; menacing, she thought, with their acidic barbs, each tree a great, single arrow aimed at the heavens.

It was dark inside the forest. Unlikely red mushrooms — like one might see in a children's picture book, one of those stories about elves — pushed through the tangle of deadfall like knobs. She picked up two branches and snapped off the twigs. They would work. She took fifty striding steps south of the cow and stabbed the first branch into the ground, then removed her blouse — white, highly visible — and hung it over top. A surrender. Then she measured fifty steps to the north of the cow, using her white slip as the other warning flag.

Finally she wrapped her jacket around her shoulders and returned to the centre. The accident scene.

The cow was beginning to smell. Soon it might draw more than flies and birds. She needed to lie down right now and stop thinking. She needed to shut off her brain at once.

*ઌ*ઌઌ

Lovilla awoke, disoriented, beneath a purple-swirled quilt in a highway motel. She'd been drooling, and yanked the quilt away from her mouth. How often were hotel quilts washed? she wondered. Who else had drooled in this same spot? She focused on her good white blouse, draped across a chair, noted the oily smudge on the shoulder and remembered that she had more to obsess about than the laundry habits of highway motels. She wasn't talking to her husband but they'd had tired sex beneath the covers — beneath, because she worried about spycams in hotel rooms and having their activities turn up on a computer screen in Belgium or Philadelphia, some pimply thirteen-year-old getting his rocks off over the sight of her boyish ass.

Roger jerked. How dare he sleep later than her after yesterday? The interview had been rescheduled; she'd have to wake him soon — two good pinches in his love handles should do it. He was sorry he'd left her so long. *Very* sorry.

What did she think her life meant? She'd thought that unanswerable, but this cow business has clinched it. Her life consisted of bizarre events and strange people. Even Roger qualified: he wore safety glasses to cut the grass. She'd stood up for a cousin who got married with a teacup on her head. Her best friend was allergic to volleyballs. Magpies and sparrows dropped, literally, at Lovilla's feet. She'd survived a Ferris wheel accident when she was ten, and had a gun pressed to her ear in a bank robbery. She babysat dead cows. I'm a receptacle for weird things, she was thinking. Crackpots, bomb-diving birds — I attract them, sparing others the trouble. A modern-day martyr. And the remarkable thing, she decided, was that no one thought her remarkable at all.

In the bank she'd known exactly what to do. Look. Listen. Pay attention to details. He wore a Levi jean jacket; the second button from the top was missing. No belt. Square hands with short, slightly tapered fingers. The nail on his right pointer was blue, as if it'd been slammed in a car door. A pinpoint indent revealed a pierced ear that had grown in. He sniffed. A lot.

It made her happy — almost to the point of bursting — that she could provide her sister with an answer now. She'd call Ara the moment they got back. She could hardly wait to invite her over, get her sitting comfortably with a mug of mocha — hot chocolate and a teaspoon of instant coffee. See her face. This is what my life means, Lovilla would say. This.

TOWARD THE MOON

THE VACATION HAD BEEN GOING REASONABLY WELL UNTIL Tommy — *Thomas*, she must watch herself now that he was fifteen and these things mattered so much more — had the mishap with the rusty nail. Now she was alone with the Heisman boy and there was rain and — oh, God! — his bare thigh only the syllable *yes* away from hers.

They were renting the cottage from Karl Robberstad, a partner in Lawrence's firm, and she had been wary from the first. "What if I drop a hot pot on the floor and burn a hole in the linoleum?"

Lawrence was peeling off his corporate identity at the end of the bed. His plaid tie was locked into its knot. "It's a bloody cabin, Susan," he had said, pawing at the noose. "They rent it a couple times every summer. Nothing will happen."

"What if I break the handle off the heirloom teapot? What if Tom has a little fire?"

Lawrence crawled into bed, free of the nuisance tie. He rolled to click off the bedside lamp. "Only a *little* fire? Why not have him burn down the whole forest?"

"What if I — "

Lawrence groaned. "Go to sleep. It's a holiday . . . we deserve it. Or would you rather we bought a tent and roughed it for two weeks? We could, you know."

The rental arrangements were made, and when the calendar page flipped to July, Susan began her To do list. Thomas had been pestering her about bringing a friend. "Two weeks is like, forever," he had said. "What am I supposed to do?" She had rattled off the usual list: fish, swim, hike, canoe, pick berries, build campfires — in truth the whole idea had been growing on her — but these were the passions of boys younger than her son, a city child who had always been more comfortable on monkey bars in concrete playgrounds than swinging from actual trees, and he would not be placated.

"Just one friend," he pleaded. "Just Reagan. He's never even been to a cottage!"

"Does it have to be him?"

"Why? What's wrong with Reagan? I thought you said he was my most polite friend. I thought you liked him." Thomas was beginning to sulk: she knew he might end up in his room for two days without speaking to her, doing God only knew what on his computer. "Besides, this is likely my last free summer."

The statement, in the end, which clinched it.

Light speed; everything was happening fast now. When he was a red and howling baby she had longed for the moment when he could articulate why his puffy fists were beating the air, why his dimpled knees were drawn to his chest. After his second birthday she dreamed of the hour she would not have to ask, "Do you need to go potty?" and he would trot off to the washroom without her, master, finally, of his own body. She mentally pushed him forward until he reached the golden age of nine — a real boy. Then she stopped gazing toward the horizon's ever greener grass.

He was, she had to accept, a middle-of-the-road child. His grades were mostly respectable Bs, he made friends easily, he was perhaps a little better than average on the soccer field. He complained when she asked him to take out the garbage or straighten his room, but he did not squirm away when she squeezed him in the kitchen, or rubbed his neck while he worked on math problems at the dining room table, or kissed him as he left for school. He had Lawrence's erect posture and sharp shoulders that narrowed to slim hips, and her milky green eyes. His chest was becoming a man's; below his knees a down of sand-coloured hair. His arms were still boyishly thin, but he would often flex his muscle and say, "Look, Mom, feel," and she would put her hand on the small bulge and tell him how strong he was becoming. She was especially fond of his mouth — he had a slight gap between his top centre teeth and turned out the most contagious smiles. He was the only person who had ever delivered her breakfast — toast, Corn Flakes, a quartered orange, strong, black coffee (she took milk) and the newspaper — in bed. The epicentre of her heart.

"He's right, you know," she told Lawrence. "Next summer he'll have a job cutting grass at a golf course or something, and every summer after there'll be work." And girls, likely, but she doesn't have to think about that now. "This *is* his last free summer."

And so that, too, was decided. But why Reagan? Of all his chums, why the one whose presence gave her a little thrill whenever she saw him coming down the walk? Was he looking for her in the window? Did he notice her shadow behind the kitchen sheers?

Reagan was a year older, but the boys were classmates. He had acquired a gift often dealt to only children, like her son: the ability to converse easily with adults. And he *was* polite. He always asked how she was and stuck around to chat. It was just that. Those small grains of attention. Charity, really. Then she would catch her reflection in the hall mirror and know she was being silly. Thirty-six years old! Shameful.

ళళళ

The cottage was a winding path through giant evergreens away from the beach. It was not what she was expecting. A few notches above rustic but not quite modern, meaning there was a toilet but you had to dip water into the pail beside it and fill the bowl before you flushed. When the water ran low you traipsed out to the public tap, filled the pail and lugged it back, slopping water on your shins. And the toilet stank.

Still, the cottage was perfectly adequate, with a large wrap-around deck where she and Lawrence lounged and read in the sun while the boys played cards on the shady side. A breeze-way took most of the sand off their feet. There were two bedrooms separated by garish floral curtains — a double bed for the adults, a set of twins with matching orange-and-brown spreads for the boys — and a large combined living and eating area ("Cool! A TV and VCR!") with a woodstove in the corner. It was neat — and comfortable enough — and they could hear the hum of motorboats and happy children from the deck. The squirrels were aggressive and frightened her — she snapped her lawnchair when they came near — but she could deal with them.

She had not anticipated the mice. Not ordinary mice, like the little gentleman in her garden — a slim, respectable-looking mouse who concerned himself with nibbling up seeds the sparrows fidgeted off their feeder — but huge, floppy rodents with white underbellies, big eyes, roundish ears, and back legs designed, she guessed, for hopping. Fat mice. She had found the first one when she nudged the barbecue out of the verandah onto the deck. "It didn't even have the decency to dart."

"I'll catch it," Lawrence promised. "It's a fluke."

"You're just saying that," she said. She had taken too much sun and her face felt like it was being stretched beyond her ears. "Where there's one there's a dozen."

"Well at least it's out here," he said, shifting beach umbrellas and air mattresses to check the corners of the verandah. "If we keep this door shut it won't get into the kitchen. I'll get a trap at the store."

"Traps," she corrected, enunciating the s. "Get traps."

Reagan found the second mouse. "I was just sitting on the can and it ran across the bathroom. I've never seen such a big one."

"Did it have a white belly?" Thomas asked.

"Yeah. And honkin' big ears."

"Oh, shit." Thomas looked up at his father. "I think it's a deer mouse."

Lawrence raised and dropped his shoulders. "So? What's the difference?"

"The difference," Thomas said, authoritatively, "is hantavirus. We talked about it in school. Basically, if you inhale deer mouse crap you bite the big one."

There was no library at the lake or, Susan learned, at the village nearest, so she gathered facts via other women on the beach. It was not easy. She felt strange — dirty, in a way — admitting they had a mouse problem, like it was the result of some familial hygienic defect. It was, she surmised, a little like confessing that you'd had scabies or lice as a child. She quickly learned about wearing gloves to collect the black pepperseed turds and where best — the consensus was kitchen cupboards — to place traps. She was cautioned, too, about the lake's bigger dangers. Bears. Forest fires further north had pushed them down to the park. "You have to be careful," the women warned beneath sun hats and striped umbrellas, bathing suit straps deliberately slid onto blushed shoulders. "Wear bells."

ৡৡৡ

"We should leave," she said. They had trapped four mice but had not seen another for two days now. She feared scampering, heard scratching. She expected a mouse would drag its tail beneath her nose while she was sleeping. "Besides, if the mice don't kill us the bears will."

But there was no insistence in her voice. Her days had fallen into a simple, sunwashed rhythm. She mooned over morning coffee on the deck. As the temperature rose she slipped into thongs, swung a beach towel around her neck and picked her way across the shady pinecone-strewn path through the trees — that forest fragrance! — to the lake.

Initially she had worn a large T-shirt over her suit, but a week had passed and she realized that she could do this — walk from the cottage to the beach uncovered: it was not a crime. Bodies spilled out of bikinis everywhere. Stretch marks glistened in the sun, pubic hair spidered down thighs, and she had even seen the leaked, sad, grey testicle of one elderly gentlemen who had parked his lawn chair close to her head. Besides, she'd "kept herself up," as one of the other mothers — younger, with two children to supervise at the water's edge — had commented. "You have a fifteen year old? Wow, you've really kept yourself up."

And then, as if to prove it, Susan went for a long swim — back and forth around the buoys — in her smooth, splashless crawl. When she came dripping out, Thomas and Reagan had pitched their towels beside hers.

"Lookin' good, Ma," Thomas said.

"Not bad for an old lady," she said, laughing, though she pulled her stomach in and felt her entire body flush. "Water's great today. You two should get in there."

Thomas, who was barely beating the sun to his Tiger Tiger ice cream cone, siphoned sand onto her leg with his free hand. She swished it off.

"Don't be a brat, Tommy." He grabbed a handful and threw it on her. "You little — " She rose to her knees and retaliated with two fists full.

Reagan reached for a child's pail — abandoned in the sand — and promptly filled it in the lake, then dumped the water over Susan's head.

"Hey, no fair! Two against one."

Then Reagan had her ankles and Thomas her wrists. They hauled her to the lake and splashed in. "One," they swung, "two, three." And she flew. A woman she had spoken to was laughing as if this was the best comedy she had seen in a long time. A trio of children had come over to watch. Far above, seagulls were acrobating across the gymnasium of sky.

"You little buggers!" Susan was wiping her eyes. She had almost lost a contact lens; she blinked it back into place. Thomas dove away from her, then began a choppy crawl toward the buoys. She buried her knees in the lake's pebbled sand: the water was level with her breasts, and very cold. "I'll get you yet!"

"Oh yeah?" Reagan was a moth's measure of distance away. She could have pushed him into the paralyzing shock of water. She could have yanked his neck down and dunked him. He was looking at her. A wet, dark-haired boy with hair under his arms, and real muscles, not the little nuggets Thomas asked her to feel. What a spectacle. There were beach sounds — seagulls, splashing, Jet Skis — but she heard none of it, with her eyes fastened to Reagan's. She was teetering on a precipice. He moved a lick of hair out of her eyes. "What are you going to do?"

❧❧❧

Lawrence wanted to have sex. She had not seen him all day; he had left early for an advertised hike with a biologist from Parks and Recreation, to learn about edible mushrooms and the medicinal uses of weeds. The boys were watching a sitcom; she thought she and Lawrence would have time before they heard the laughtrack end. And she needed it. Oh, Lord.

There was something about the cottage, with its old blankets and musty smell, the bedroom's thick darkness. Even the canned laughter, the boys' proximity made her hot. *Oh yeah? What are you going to do?* And then his fingers. Touching her. So bold!

It didn't take long, for either of them.

"Thanks," she said, she *always* said after Lawrence satisfied her.

"No, thank *you*."

This was their little ritual.

"Are you getting up?" he asked. "I could use a Kleenex here."

She scaled across him and slipped into the socks she kept on top of the covers — no more mice, but she was not taking chances with bare feet. She swept the curtain aside. The bathroom was only a few steps away, with a real door. Down the short hall, past the boys' room, the television's protean light played beneath the curtain. She returned with the Kleenex.

"Better tell those kids to get some sleep, hey? I told them we'd go fishing bright and early tomorrow," Lawrence said.

"How early?" She was enjoying the late mornings. She was getting used to her laziness.

"Six."

She curled into Lawrence — her front to his back, her nose in his hair, and slept without her usual panicked dream about racing for an airplane in a strange airport and almost missing her flight.

ଐଐଐ

The fishing trip was a success. They were able to rent a boat at one of the park's smaller, adjacent lakes and buy temporary licenses for Lawrence and Reagan; Thomas wouldn't need one for another year.

"I caught the biggest one," Thomas said, beaming. He held his string of pickerel and northern pike up for her camera.

"Now one of you all together," she insisted, wanting to capture the perfection of the morning on each of their faces. Lawrence stepped into the middle. "It takes me a long time to focus," she said, adjusting the manual aperture. "Say 'fish fry.'"

"Fish fry," Lawrence and Thomas said. Reagan, shirtless, barefoot, in jeans with wet, sandy hems, offered a high-kilowatt smile.

❧❧❧

The day before the accident, Susan was preparing for company.

Lawrence had met a couple on the nature hike — Albertans, with a fifth wheel trailer wedged into a campsite and two grown kids at home — and invited them for a barbecue. "Just burgers," he had said. "Nothing fancy."

"Can we bring anything?" Jan had asked. Jan was the man, not the woman. Tan shorts and sturdy shoes, and he walked with purpose, like a Boy Scout leader. Susan thought his thick, drooping mustache made him look like a muskrat. "A salad . . . some beer?"

"You don't have to," Lawrence had said, "but you can if you want."

Susan could tell that her husband liked this man, Jan, and his pleasant wife, Sherry (or Michelle, or Linda — she would have to ask Lawrence again). She was not keen on hosting a meal — even a hamburger meal — but Lawrence liked so few people. He was not, actually, a friendly sort. It was good to see him having fun, making friends, she thought. The least she could do was throw a few burgers on the barbie.

There was beer during, and more after. Jan and Kathy — at least she'd had the era right, if not the name — made a foul-tasting lager just short of molasses that Susan accidentally spilled into the sand. Lawrence was letting the boys split a beer. He was loosening up. Someone put on a Blue Rodeo CD, then Thomas emerged from the cottage with lawn darts. It was the women and Thomas against the rest.

"Aren't these things illegal now?" Kathy asked. No one could remember the rules to the game, so they made their own. Their team was losing, but there was still a faint flame of hope.

"Illegal?" Susan was aiming for the yellow plastic ring. She lobbed the dart, missing her target but nailing the neighbour's canoe. "I don't think so."

"Lawrence," Jan said, "you're a man of the law, what do you think?"

Lawrence shrugged. "Beats me. Maybe they're just illegal in Alberta.

One of those boundary things, like the rats."

"What about rats?" Thomas asked.

"There's not supposed to be any in Alberta," Susan said. She sipped the syrupy homebrew. She had not spilled enough. "They've got a rat patrol."

"It's true," Kathy said, "we don't have any rats."

"But how can you be sure?" Susan thwacked the soil off a dart.

"Yeah," Thomas jumped in, "do they have guards armed with slingshots at the border or something?"

Laughter rolled like smoke toward the tops of the pines. Lawrence threw a wild dart, narrowly missing the cottage.

"I think I remember something about some kid getting a dart stuck in his eye, but I don't — "

"It wasn't his eye," Reagan interjected. His dart sailed. Bull's eye. "It was his heart. And he died."

Kathy laughed through her nose. "That's just one of those — oh, what do they call them — urban myths?"

"No, it's a fact," Thomas said. "I heard about it, too."

"It *is* true," Reagan said, defensively. The conversation turned serious. He hadn't said much of anything all night.

❧❧❧

Lawrence built a campfire. Susan was in the kitchen, microwaving popcorn, when Kathy burst through the squeaking screen door. "Where's the washroom?"

Susan pointed. "Behind that curtain and to your left. There's a real door." She thought of saying something about the water and flushing, but surely Kathy would figure it out. The microwave beeped and she removed the popcorn. She cautiously — *still* cautiously — opened the bottom cupboard for a bowl. Footsteps behind her.

"Excuse me." Reagan's hand lit on her hip while he shimmied past. "Smells good."

"Does it ever," Kathy said, returning. She lifted the box and read. "Microwave Light. Should we add extra butter?"

Reagan slipped behind the curtain, to the bathroom, Susan supposed. Kathy was into the fridge for the margarine. She scooped three lumps into Susan's waiting bowl. "You are aware," Kathy said, "that that boy has the serious hots for you."

"What . . . Reagan?" She emphasized her incredulity with a chuckle. "I don't think so." She turned and slid the bowl into the microwave. A phantom hand warmed her neck.

"Couldn't keep his eyes off you when we were eating, or while we were playing lawn darts." Kathy rinsed the spoon and shook it before setting it in the plastic rack to dry.

"No way. Cripes, I could be his mother! He's even got a girlfriend."

This last bit wasn't true, as far as she knew, but it sounded good.

"Well, I'm just callin' 'em like I — "

"Popcorn ready?" Thomas was in the doorway, half in, half out. Susan didn't think he'd heard anything. Her son smelled of smoke.

"We're coming out right now."

Back at the fire she wondered about acoustics. Reagan had been a long time in the cottage, and now had wandered down the sandy road, hands arrowed into pockets, alone toward the moon. How much had he heard behind the curtain?

❧❧❧

The Albertans returned to Alberta. The men swapped business cards but Lawrence left Jan's on the coffee table beneath a newspaper and Susan pitched the works into the woodstove. No one had definite plans for the day. The radio said to expect temperatures in the low thirties; a dip in the lake would be necessary.

Susan was deliberating over bathing suits. The mainly blue, high-cut maillot that tied around her neck and best emphasized her legs? The strapless yellow one-piece that offset her tan? Or the red-and-white striped bikini she had not yet had the confidence — or the audacity — to wear? She put the latter on and twisted before the full-length mirror. Things hadn't started to fall yet. She could still do this. Her stomach was white compared to the rest of her, her fingers tanned against it, as if she were two people. Yes, that's what she'd say if Lawrence asked why, after so many years of camouflaging her body in what could be described as matronly suits — she owned one with a pleated skirt that effectively hid her thighs — she was now hitting the beach in a bikini worthy of *Sports Illustrated*.

Lawrence did not ask. He had discovered a clump of bear scat — "Just like Saskatoon berry pie filling!" — behind the cottage and was off to report it to Parks and Rec. He would find out if there was any real danger.

"And the mice . . . " she called after him. "Ask about the deer mice."

Thomas and Reagan were eating cereal in front of the television when she entered the room. "Morning," she said, effecting casualness by cleaning sleep from her eye with her ring finger and yawning.

"Morning, Mom." Thomas did not look up from the screen.

Reagan did. "Hi, Susan." She felt his eyes on her back as she slipped a slice of whole wheat bread into the toaster. Who did she think she was fooling? She had not chosen the bikini to tan her belly, and she had not experimented with her hair every morning — pulling it back, letting it fall forward over one eye — because she was interested in a new style. She was playing a game — with a boy, her son's friend — and it was . . . well, she decided . . . it was pathetic. But how could she stop it now? The ball was rolling. She liked that he looked at her breasts when he set his bowl in the sink, and again when he poured her a second cup of coffee.

Everything was twisted, and surreal, and somehow better here at the lake, including sex with Lawrence. She suspected Reagan knew he was inside her head now. The acknowledgement was out there, and with it came a pinch of relief.

She sat at the end of the table, one leg beneath her, and forced a necessary calm. "What are you doing today?"

"We're taking the bikes out," he said, sitting kittycorner. "Wanna come?"

"No . . . I . . . I'm just going to stick around here. Finish my book. Swim." He looks so dejected, she thought. "But thanks, maybe we'll all do something later."

"Okay," he said, and when he got up, he bumped her knee with his own and left a handprint of warmth on her neck. This time it was real.

❧❧❧

She was never quite sure how Thomas got his foot nailed to a scrap piece of two-by-four. It was dusk. Probably he was just poking about in the pile behind the cottage — who knew why? — and stepped in the wrong place. He hopped back to them, not quite crying but not quite in control either. When Susan saw the board nailed to his foot she swooned.

"Jesus," Lawrence said, letting his son fall onto him as he bent to inspect the mess. It wasn't bleeding much yet. The bleeding began when Lawrence tried to pull the board out.

"Should I find some Tylenol? How about a cold washcloth?" Susan was dizzy. She did not cope well with injuries, and there had, blessedly, been few to cope with in their lives. She ran and grabbed a bottle of Tylenol, a glass of water and a cold, wet facecloth. Thomas had hobbled into a lawnchair, foot still firmly nailed to the board. He was very pale. Reagan stood beside him but concentrated on Lawrence, as if awaiting instructions from a chief. They were all stunned. It was like a drop sheet had fallen to stifle them.

"I've got to take him in, Sue. It's deep. And that's a rusty nail."

"Oh, God," Susan said.

"There's a hospital in town. It's only fifty K or so. We'll get him looked after." There was no argument about who would drive; Susan had never learned how.

"But what about that board? Are you just going to leave it?" If it had been anyone else but her son she might have laughed at the sight of a piece of raw wood nailed to a foot. But this was her son! This was Thomas!

"It looks like we have to. For now. Give me those things." He took the bottle of painkillers and shook out eight. He gave Thomas three, took two himself and put the rest in his pocket. "You stay here and settle down," he said. "I'll take care of this."

"Should I come?" Reagan asked.

Lawrence checked Susan: one hand over her eyes and the other flat against the cottage's wall, as if that alone was preventing her from falling. "You're better off here." He bent toward Reagan. "Take care of her."

❧❧❧

"Is there anything on?" She had mostly avoided being alone with him. First she had said she needed a nap (she tucked in but didn't sleep), then she went for a walk and did not ask him along. When it began to rain there was nowhere to go but back. She worried that this little tragedy was making her rude, and she did not want that, either. She sat on the couch. Reagan had the lumpy chair with the sprung springs.

"Just some old movie. Here," he said, passing the remote control. "You try."

She flicked through the channels. There were only three. "Guess this is about the best," she said, returning to the movie. It seemed to be a comedy, which was reassuring. She set the remote on the coffee table and curled her legs — still bare, despite the sodden night — beneath her.

"Aren't you cold?" he asked.

She felt her skin prickle. "Not bad."

He rose and took the blanket off the end of the couch, half placed and half threw it over top of her. "Better?"

"Thanks," she said. They watched the movie, but it was hard to get into it without knowing the characters or the premise. It would have been hard if she *had* known the characters and premise. "I could use a beer."

"I'll get you one."

What an eager young man, this Heisman boy. She wanted to make him happy, and if that meant letting him fetch her a beer or cover her legs, so be it. They weren't breaking any laws. "And you can get yourself one, too." Now, she thought, we're breaking laws.

The movie was there, between them, something to fall back on when neither could think of anything to say. "What could be taking them so long?" she wondered.

"The rain," Reagan answered. "It's really coming down." After he delivered the beer he had not returned to his seat. He had taken the west end of the couch, but was now closer to the middle. How had it happened, this creeping? If Lawrence and Thomas returned right now, would it look suspicious, or natural? It really was the best angle from which to watch the show. Still, she had the feeling that she should get out of there. It was nonsense. She could imagine, years from now, Reagan telling this tale and spiralling away from the truth. "She was thirty-six — a cougar! — but, man, she didn't look it. She didn't *act* it, if you know what I mean." She would not allow herself to become the fodder for some locker room joke. Even if he was genuinely in love with her at this moment. Even if she could imagine their first kiss and his hands tentatively exploring beneath the blanket.

"I'm off to bed," she said, but before she made the motion of going, his hand was on her leg, just above her bare knee.

"Thanks for the beer."

❧❧❧

"I didn't know if he'd had a tetanus shot," Lawrence was saying. They had returned a half hour after she had left Reagan—left Reagan's hand—on the couch. "So they gave him one, just to be safe."

"That's good," she said. "Better to be safe."

Thomas was in bed, his foot wrapped in gauze. He had kept the board — but not the nail — as a gruesome souvenir. The boys were talking quietly in the other room.

"What about the crutches?"

"We have to drop them off on our way back to the city. He may not even need them after tomorrow. And we're gone the day after that."

"Yes. I'm starting to gear up for it," she said, sleepily. "Talk to you in the morning."

He kissed her cheek. Then they slept.

જ્જ્જ્

Lawrence returned from the Visitor Centre with a pamphlet on Hantavirus Pulmonary Syndrome, and Susan discovered that Thomas had been right: the disease is transmitted when dust containing infected rodent shit is inhaled. She read and reread. It is fatal to almost half the people who contract it. The pamphlet advised wetting turds with a disinfectant before handling them.

What Lawrence found out about the bears he kept to himself. Susan blamed him for this. It was something she would flag over his head for a long time after. They were black bears, though black bears could be brown and that was what they had about thirty yards in front of them, between their cottage — the Robberstads' cottage — and the store.

"It's only got three legs!" Thomas cried, leaning on his crutch. He was down to one now. And tomorrow was home. "I wonder what happened to it."

A crowd had gathered to watch the bear swat garbage around. It was adept at finding the good stuff — pizza crusts, steak bones — and leaving the undesired — used Pampers, pop bottles — alone. Lawrence thought someone should alert Parks staff. Susan said she thought someone had already done just that.

"There they come," Reagan said. He was closest to her, but she did not feel it now. It was already passing, as these things — whatever they were — sometimes did if left alone. A brown truck pulled up and two identically dressed men — tan suits, caps, work boots — jumped out. The passenger had a gun. A little girl started to cry. There were several grunts of disapproval and one person, a teen in baggy shorts and basketball shoes, clapped and yelled, "Whoo hoo!"

"But surely they're not going to — " Susan could not believe the drama unfolding before them. She felt completely powerless.

"Must be a stun gun," Lawrence said, though she sensed his doubt.

"I don't think so," Reagan said. "Looks like the real thing."

The Parks officer fired a shot into the air. Somebody screamed. Seagulls squawked. The bear turned. It faced the officer, but it did not move toward him.

"I've heard about this bear," Lawrence said in Susan's ear. "It's been causing a lot of trouble in the campground. It's just not safe to let it roam around."

"But cripes, they're not going to — " She could not even say it.

"All right, stand back everyone," the other, gunless officer was saying. He was pushing the crowd back, though as soon as he turned, people crept forward again, like they were playing a schoolyard game.

Another shot rang through the air. And the bear fell. The two wardens and a tourist dragged the dead bear by its three legs and wrestled it into the half-ton's box.

"All right folks, show's over." The Parks staff returned to the truck and began driving away, but they had left the gate open and the bystanders saw the bear lying there, like an overgrown stuffed animal that someone had won at a fair.

"Jesus," Lawrence said. He quickly turned and hiked toward the cottage. Reagan followed.

Only Susan and Thomas were left. Everyone, even the boy who had cheered, had gone on to something else now. Susan walked over to her son and wrapped her arm around his waist.

"I wish I hadn't seen that," Thomas said, and she thought he had never seemed sadder. She hugged her boy then, and he hugged her back. She helped get him turned around — his other crutch — and they made their silent, careful way back to the Robberstads' cottage. He had grown taller, her son, her Thomas, in these two weeks, and she had only now noticed. He had passed her by a mile.

WINTERING

"HAVE YOU CARVED THE PUMPKIN YET?" DOMINIQUE IS IN THE kitchen, unloading groceries. Groceries that *she* bought with *her* money, which she'll no doubt remind me about before this Halloween day is done.

"Just getting to it," I call from my office. "I've been working." I flick on my computer, pull an old story onto the screen. Anything will do. My wife wouldn't know new from old; she wouldn't look that closely.

In the kitchen she slams cupboard drawers, then pounds across the dining room to my office on the other side. "Jesus, Pete. I've been asking you to get on that for two days already. It's tonight, you know. Where's Tina?" She stamps out and calls our daughter, who won't call back because she's playing at the neighbour's.

I let her search for a moment, then yell: "She's at the neighbour's!" I turn off the computer and head for the kitchen where a pumpkin awaits its face. "They're having a party. I told you about it last night." I dig in the cutlery drawer for a suitable knife.

Dominique's gone upstairs and I'm not sure if she hears me. I make the first slice. When she returns she's shed her short skirt, blazer and silk blouse for stovepipe jeans and a Toronto Blue Jays sweatshirt, but she's forgotten to take off

191

the oversized earrings that match the suit. "What were you yelling?"

"I said she's at the party next door. We talked about it last night." I've spread newspapers across the kitchen table, gutted the pumpkin, and am working on one mangled eye when I feel her, glaring over my shoulder.

"You should be doing this with Tina," she says. "I'm going to call her."

I finish the first eye and proceed to the second. They are not parallel, which I hope will add to the effect. One will look down, the other up. A lazy eye pumpkin.

Dominique's on the phone to the neighbour. I tune in and out. "Yes . . . a long day . . . the Quebec referendum."

My wife is the news director at a rock 'n' roll radio station. Until yesterday, when the future of a united Canada was dangling from a high wire, her world was dominated by the referendum, but now that the votes have been counted and the "*Non*" side has won by a sliver, it will revert back to civic squabbles and police chases.

The kids who listen to her station do not listen for the news, presented in tiny capsules at thirty-minute intervals, and the station owners are reacting in kind. There's been talk of cutbacks; Dominique may lose two of her prodigies. That revelation, plus the uncertainty that's rocked the country over the past several months, plus the sad fact that her husband hasn't earned a cheque since February, have all shown themselves in a new crease across her forehead. She's taken to wearing her bangs down now, rather than combing them off to the side and spraying them in place. I wonder if her lover has noticed the change, or if this is something only a husband of nine years would pick up on.

"She'll be home in ten minutes," Dominique says, hanging up, "but you better carry on. I know how long these things take you."

"Of course you'd have it carved in five minutes," I say. I have pumpkin pulp on my hand; I wing it onto the newspaper.

"Four," she says, hands braced on the hips that continue to appeal to me. I know this stance. I know this tilt of her head, this tone of voice.

"And it would look like shit."

She fills the big pot with water. "You could have at least started supper. It's not enough that I buy the groceries, but I work all day then have to come home and cook, too."

"I told you, I was working." I'm having trouble with the left eye. I've cut out far too much. I hear the crack as Dominique breaks a handful of spaghetti in half, then the plop as she drops it into the pot. It'll only be a matter of minutes before she remarks on the power bill I stuck to the fridge.

"Ninety-four dollars! Thank God *someone* in this house has a job."

There. She's said it. A half turn of the knife already deeply imbedded back there. I slash through the pumpkin to create a mouth, a perfect oval to let the scream out.

❧❧❧

Every afternoon at 3:15, a little man skirts past my window, scratching his chin and looking pensive. Although it's late November and Saskatchewan, his light jacket is unzipped and he does not protect his head. His hands, when not scratching his stubbly chin, are stuffed into the jacket pockets. I see that his wrists are small, even frail, like sparrows' wings. A harmless eccentric; there used to be several in this neighbourhood, an old area, near City Hospital and the river.

He walks like a Geisha girl. I'll give him a dog and a ramshackle basement suite, littered with empty chip bags and bottles. A friend named Dave who has to pound on his door eight times before he answers, because he's busy with his dog, Pogey. The Geisha girl man is training Pogey to play the harmonica. He's fastened the dented instrument to a length of wire, which he's looped over the small dog's head. So far, it's not going well.

I push the button that turns my screen off. I am beginning to loathe November, for no one reason in particular. It should be a good month to "buckle down," as Dominique says, to "get focused." Today I am focused on three facts: I am a husband, a father and a writer of unsuccessful stories, not necessarily in that order. My wife is having an affair with a stockbroker named Les and my daughter is being brought up by someone else. Tina spends mornings in kindergarten and afternoons in daycare. At times the guilt of having her in daycare while I'm supposedly creating successful stories is too much, and I contemplate giving it all up in favour of what Dominique refers to as a real job.

But not yet.

Besides, I am not without meagre success. Three years ago a reviewer — in the *Globe and Mail*, no less — gushed about my second collection of stories, stating that I possessed "a chameleon talent for creating colourful characters in ever-changing environs." Others critics predicted that my work-in-progress would secure me a coveted place in the upper echelons of Canadian literature. That much-awaited collection is still more locked inside me than in the manila folder on my desk. The chameleon, it seems, has crept on. In its absence I've enjoyed several long, lazy afternoons of tiddling away at the piano. I've attended many a "meeting" with my cohorts at the Senator Hotel. I've hidden under whatever rock's available.

Dominique says I don't live, I subsist. She says I have an uncanny knack for it, subsisting. It's true. Thus far I've survived on small honorariums, the royalties from the two mildly successful books, and the occasional godsend grant from the Canada Council. She never used to mind. She used to tell the story herself of how on the night of March 15th, 1989, I cashed a two hundred dollar advance and succeeded to squander the entire amount on several rounds with strangers at the pub. She used to laugh about it.

The computer, blind without its flashing cursor, hums contentedly. Sometimes this soft sound puts me to sleep, right here at my desk. My office is adequate, with room enough for a six-foot fig tree, my wrap-around desk and chair, a lamp, small table and a reading chair, where Tina curls up on my knee with her books.

The room is surrounded on three sides by tall windows that do not open. The twisted vines of a derelict Virginia creeper obscure my view on one side. Through the south windows I look out onto the street, and beyond that, to the corner store parking lot and two newspaper recycling bins. I once confiscated a thousand unused envelopes from that bin, most of which I still have, in boxes, in the basement. The west windows frame the avenue and my neighbours' tidy houses.

In the daytime this is a quiet block. Most are at work, and the children, of which there are several more each year as retired neighbours reluctantly move to seniors' highrises

(I believe the cliché "dragged kicking and screaming" actually does apply here) and a new generation moves in, are either infants or school-aged. I miss the old man across the street who got up at six o'clock to cut his grass. His wife trimmed the edges of the lawn with scissors. Now professionals are taking over the neighbourhood, and it scares me. Professors, engineers, a theologian, a podiatrist. There are no more two and a half storey houses that advertise "Suites for Rent" in their windows. Seven years ago, when Dominique and I bought our corner house, I blended in. Painters and writers occupied the top floors of these rental houses, but one by one, the houses were sold, renovated and resold; my friends displaced.

I stare at my computer screen, where I have typed an opening sentence:"I suppose this would be a good time to tell you I don't love you anymore."These are the words I expect to hear every day, the words whispered through my dreams. Dominique has made no apology for her affair, and, what's worse, it's not just sex.

If Tina has noticed her mother's preoccupation of late she's keeping it inside. Inside is where she and I stay while Dominique is off cavorting most week nights and Saturday evenings. I don't wait up.

"I suppose this would be a good time to tell you I don't love you anymore." I want to build a story around this line but I'm blocked. I've been blocked for many months, never getting beyond the first few paragraphs of a new idea. The stories I sent out in the spring have been coming back rejected, like hate mail."You deliberately wrote a non-story." "We suggest you take a writing course.""Trees died for this??" One nasty editor, a man whose own book I reviewed for a literary journal years ago and who has apparently not yet lived it down, wrote:"This has all the symptoms of AIDS."

In particular, editors have been stressing the lack of physical description in my work, my tendency to wash over characters and story lines like a child's primitive drawing. My characters are all neuroses.There are no fingers. No ear lobes.

There have been other times during my writing life when I've felt I've lost it, but those times it always came back.This time I fear it's gone for good. I no longer have the patience, the desire to dig deep into my psyche or wherever else it is one goes to retrieve the past, pontificate on the present, speculate on the future, disguise it and slap it all down so someone can tear it apart.

Perhaps it's my age.At forty-three, I've stopped playing the game. I've had it with the pretentious literary crowd I was once so enamoured with. Bookstore readings, university lectures, the library circuit; ultimately tedious, and there's no place for a fat forty-three-year-old among all those controversial and articulate young writers who have their first books published before they've had their first knock-down-drag-out hangover.

Forty-three is fat, lying low and balding. It's never picking up the ringing phone for fear it'll be someone wanting something from me. It's being supported by a wife in full-blown love with a stockbroker; the mother of our child dragging my name through the gutter any chance she gets; a bright, coiffured, upwardly mobile woman who's just waiting for the right moment to get the hell out of Dodge.

I delete the sentence I've been mesmerized by for several minutes. Maybe the little man will become my saving grace. Maybe Pogey will learn a few notes on the harmonica, and the pair will busk downtown in front of the Midtown Plaza. I sit and wait for the words, fingers ready, but nothing happens. It's just not there.

ๆๆๆๆ

December. Dominique, in bra and leggings, is packing sweaters into our burgundy luggage set, a wedding gift from my sister. "Pete, it's work."

"Work? A four-day ski trip to Whitefish?"

She zips the suitcase shut and buckles it up. "It's a client appreciation thing. You know we do something every year for the ones who spend the most." She heaves the crammed suitcase off the bed and sets it near the door.

"I suppose Les is going."

She slides her arms into the sleeves of a black turtleneck, then ducks her head through. "There are four of us from the station and four clients, and yes, Les is one of them."

I swirl the ice cubes in my five o'clock drink. Tina's playing dolls in her room across the hall, so I'm careful to keep my voice down. "What about Tina? How long's it been since you gave that kid sixty consecutive minutes of your time?"

"Tina's fine." Dominique brushes out her auburn hair, then pulls it back in a ponytail, which makes her look younger, perky. "She's a bright, well-adjusted — "

"You missed her Christmas concert for fuck's sake!"

Dominique doesn't say anything, but there's a sharp intake of breath. It was unforgivable that she wasn't there, and she knows it. "I'm sorry about that. You know I was held up. There'll be other concerts."

"There'll never be another *first* concert!" I finish the last of my drink, and push the suitcase out of the doorway into

198

the hall so I can close the door. "Don't even pretend you've ever been her mother. She's an inconvenience. That's all either of us has ever been to you. Baggage."

Dominique reaches for the doorknob but I block her.

"You son of a bitch. Don't you dare tell me what kind of a mother I am."

She screws her face up against mine. "I work fifty, even sixty hours a week so there'll be food on the table, gas in the car, a mortgage payment made at the end of the month." She jabs me in the chest. "I work so you can sit at home and pretend to be writing the great Canadian novel."

She pushes me aside, opens the door and goes to Tina. I hear her tell our daughter that she's going away for a few days, and that Daddy's going to take her to McDonalds for supper. Tomorrow maybe he'll take her tobogganing. Won't that be fun?

A car honks twice and I walk to the window. My wife's cab awaits.

ֆֆֆ

The talk show host is introducing two men who've been raped by women. I didn't know this was physically possible and have to watch. Earlier, on the news at noon, I watched a segment on a Vancouver artist who's been accused of promoting pornography through her nude paintings. At least three of the fastest rising stars in Canadian literature are former prostitutes.

Well, that's one way. I could, for example, exploit the casual friendship I have with the podiatrist's wife next door. It's not even a friendship, really. We say hello. We've batted the weather, that favourite Saskatchewan topic, back and forth across the snowy hedge that separates our yards.

She is quite beautiful. I could exploit her long, smooth neck, that noble head held high like a race horse. Blue eyes that could slice a heart into thin slivers, like an onion.

She's studying art history, slings a green campus knapsack across her shoulder and walks to the university. Her golden hair is always free, flying, as she propels those shapely legs past my house.

I could take ten years off her thirty, erase the fact that she has a six-year-old son whom Tina plays with. Give her a lover, the university professor, much younger than her doctor husband, who, because he doesn't get any at home, places ads in dirty magazines. *Hi, I'm a professional and my name is John. I'm looking for women heavily into masturbation, phone sex, toys. I like to take Polaroids and videos. Write me. Box #11938.*

In my mind I block and delete the whole thing, then take a sip of my beer, gone warm in the glass. Tina will be home from daycare soon. I've only got a few more minutes alone before Mrs. Murphy drops her off. I'll enjoy them at my window perch. I could sit like this all day. I often do. Who needs television, with so much going on outside every window? People just don't look. Too busy, or maybe they're afraid. Maybe they think all the action will make them dizzy, like one of those merry-go-rounds in the park where I take Tina. Maybe they think they'll fall off.

The Geisha girl man is fifteen minutes late today. He shuffles past just as the school bus drops off students by the recycling bins. A band of loud boys, exaggerating his walk, pursue him down the street. I stand up and crane my neck for a better look. The little man continues down the street looking very much like a donkey, the ragtag group behind like those donkey boys in *Pinocchio*. One boy is having a real go at him. A large hunk of a kid who will lose his baby fat in a few months and take to breaking windshields with baseball bats. Give him a few years and even his own mother won't trust him.

They are almost out of my sight now. Something inside me wants to chase after them, to bring the feeble man into my home and protect him from this adolescent wrath, but then Mrs. Murphy pulls up with Tina. I see her reach across the back seat to unlock my daughter's door. Someone at the daycare, maybe Mrs. Murphy, maybe her helper, has gathered Tina's long hair in a ponytail high on her head. It flaps as she runs toward the house.

I hoist myself out of the chair to greet her at the side door.

"Papa!" she says, and throws her snow-frosted arms around my neck. I don't know why she calls me that. I'm much more a "Dad," or "Daddy." Too much *Hansel and Gretel*, I guess. We've collected a rather large number of children's books since Tina was born. She loves the classic fairy tales, and I don't mind reading them over and over again.

"How was your day, Sweetheart?" I undo the scarf, pull off the parka.

"Great! We made snowflakes. See?" She opens her backpack and pulls out a handful of paper snowflakes, some mere accidents with scissors.

I admire her handiwork and together we tape the flimsy snowflakes to the window. "There," I say, "doesn't that look pretty?"

"Uh huh," she says, brushing her bangs from her eyes and looking up as if to ask what's next. "Is Mom coming home for supper?"

"Not tonight, Honey. She's working late."

"Oh." She flicks on the television.

"You know what I'm going to do? I'm going to make a big fire in the fireplace and order a pizza for supper."

"Okay."

We spread a blanket on the living room rug, then I build the fire and watch the flames eat the first draft of an ancient story.

Tina, at the window, calls: "He's here! Pizza man's here!"

After our picnic we feed our paper plates to the fire. We read. *Sleeping Beauty*, *Peter Pan*, *The Emperor's New Clothes*.

Tina falls asleep on the couch. A snowflake flutters off the window.

❧❧❧

Dominique is in Mexico. Indefinitely. Her note said that she'd left the radio station and the marriage, and our divorce is on the immediate horizon.

I am making breakfast for Tina, who's hunched over in her chair at the table, her chin propped on her fist. She could be asleep but her slippered feet, swinging below the chair, prove otherwise. "Where's Mexico, Papa?" "I'll show you," I say, taking her hand and leading her into my office. Years ago, when I first I embarked on my dubious journey as a writer, I surrounded myself with accoutrements, thinking, foolishly, that their presence might inspire me. An expensive letter opener with a loon carved at one end; a gold pen set; marble bookends to keep my reference books in place. I also purchased a globe — it lights up when it's plugged in. I give it a spin. "Mexico is here," I say, pointing.

"Is it far away?" She runs her finger over the topographical surface, feeling all the ridges.

"Very far away. We live here," I point out our dot in the middle of the Prairies, "and Mommy's all the way down here, where there's no snow at all."

"Does it look like the postcard?" Tina asks, referring to the beach scene that arrived from Cancun two weeks ago.

"Yes. It looks just like that."

The toaster buzzes and we return to the kitchen. I pop up two slices. "Just peanut butter, right?"

"Uh huh."

We've settled into a comfortable routine, Tina and I. Up at 8:00 and at the table by 8:15, where we eat toast and slurp hot chocolate together. By 8:30 Tina's bundled up and ready for Mrs. Murphy, who picks her up and takes her to kindergarten. I don't write for the next seven and a half hours and we meet again at four o'clock. Weekends are walks in the park, "Chopsticks" on the piano. McDonalds and Saturday morning cartoons. On a scale of one to ten, I'd say I'm operating at about an eight.

The podiatrist's wife says I'm adjusting well, but the truth is it's so much easier now. I don't wonder when Dominique will be home. I don't have to listen to her daily diatribes. I can breathe.

Tina is a neat kid, a surprise package. On our weekend excursion to the art gallery, she asked to throw a coin in the wishing well. I had a nickel and a dime in my pocket. We closed our eyes and threw them. As we walked home through the snow, too thin to be called beautiful, I asked her what she wished for. "World peace," she said, fitting her gloved hand into mine. "What about you?"

❧❧❧

On February first my estranged wife calls. I refuse to wake Tina, who's fallen asleep in my bed. The connection is bad. "I'll be home in three days," she says. "I'm putting the house up. I'm willing to split with you on it even though I paid for most of it myself. I think that's being overly generous but I don't want to haggle over anything with lawyers. Oh, and Pete, have Tina's stuff ready."

I've feared this was coming, did not expect it so soon. I carry Tina to her own bed and stumble on an errant picture book. *Pinocchio*. Tina loves the timeless characters: the benevolent shoemaker and the giant fish that swallowed the poor puppet. I tuck her under the covers and kiss her warm cheek. I pick the book off the floor on my way out.

Downstairs, in my office, I settle into my reading chair and light a cigarette, a habit I've taken up again in the month that Dominique's been away. *Pinocchio* rests in my lap. I open and read about the poor puppet who makes a career out of screwing up. I read it again, and a third time.

It's so simple; I don't know why I've never thought of it before. I could do this. I could write children's books. The market's guaranteed, and I could make children happy. What could be more important than that?

I close the book, light another cigarette and look up to the doorway, expecting to see Dominique, or at least her shadow as she crosses against the light. I can almost smell her, hear her 'tck' her tongue against the roof of her mouth. "I'll start in the morning," I say, as if she is right there, leaning against the door frame, arms crossed below her breasts, watching and judging as she so often has. "Promise."

IN THE LAND OF HEALING WATERS

NONA IS HERE BECAUSE OF HER BONES. THE SPA, THE MASSAGES — they seem to help her bad back, the beginning stages of osteoporosis.

"It's lovely, isn't it?"

"What?" She turns. A woman in a yellow bathing cap is creeping through the water toward her; it's the most practical way to travel around the pool. "Oh . . . the water, yes." With the absence of hair it's impossible to determine how old this woman might be, but she's a senior, surely, her face, like Nona's, becoming soft as dough. She has counted twenty-three bodies in the large indoor spa, and only one, she guesses, could name the top ten songs on the radio. The lifeguard, a spongy fellow who looks all of thirteen, occasionally glances up from his magazine and surveys the aging patrons — mostly women, which is to be expected — with a grimace of pure disgust. She doubts he'd be of much use if any one of them dared have a medical emergency.

Nona is sitting with her back against a jet where water bubbles out with a force that makes a real difference to her bones, especially at the intersection between tailbone and pelvis. The woman with the yellow dome sits on the concrete underwater ledge — the bench, of sorts — beside her. "Have you been here before?" she asks Nona.

"No. This is my first time. My son bought me a three-day package. He thought that since his wife's parents like it, I would, too." Oh, dear. She supposes that sounded a bit snappy, when really she was so pleased with Gerry's birthday gift. "Have you come before?"

"Oh, yes," the woman says brightly. She cups the water, lets it drain through her ringless fingers. "I try to come twice a year. A little treat for myself."

She has a pleasant voice. Nona imagines that she may have been a teacher, or perhaps a nurse. In their day that's what most of them went through for.

"Where are you from?" the woman asks.

"Warman," Nona answers, "a small community just north of Saskatoon — "A *bedroom* community, that's what they say, but the term makes her uncomfortable.

"Oh, I know it. It seems like a nice place to live. Quiet."

"Yes," Nona agrees, looking at her feet. Sitting is a chore. Her feet and knees keep rising to the surface. She's embarrassed that her toenails aren't in better shape. She'll have to use her pedicure coupon later, if this is how it's going to be, feet always poking out for anyone's inspection. They give up on sitting and grasp the plastic tubing that runs along the perimeter of the deck. Reclined and fully floating now, except for tilted heads and elbows out by their ears, they stare up at the ceiling. A strange way to conduct a conversation, Nona thinks, but if they roll onto their stomachs it will be bums floating up. Bums and heels. "We farmed near Warman, and when Don passed away it just made sense to move to town."

"Oh, so you farmed." The woman draws her knees up — first one, then the other — in a pedalling motion that Nona supposes is good exercise. "Did you enjoy it?"

Now there was a question! An odd one, especially coming from a stranger. In all her years, she can't recall anyone asking it. *Enjoy* it? Well, sure she enjoyed it. She loved the space and the acre of garden — though that did get a bit much — and having Don always close to home. In their forty-two years together they'd spent only five nights apart — three when she gave birth to Gerry, another when she lost the second baby, and one more when Don had the gallbladder operation. "But that was done using a laser, not the old way, and he was practically in and out."

"Pardon me?"

Oh, dear. Has she spoken out loud? "Um . . . nothing." She probably thinks I'm an old fool. "I was just . . . remembering."

A sign advises a twenty-minute maximum in the hot pool, and Nona is sure she's been in all of that, but it's not even particularly hot and it's nice having someone to chat with. She's never been one to start conversations — Don had been the talker — but if anyone speaks to her she tries to keep the volley going. It's only polite.

"By the way, my name's Chris," the woman says, turning to face Nona now. Yes, Nona thinks, taking her first good look at the pleasant woman floating eight inches away. She looks like a Chris, like one of those self-assured women who finds a way to enjoy whatever life throws at her. She has a clear, open face with a spray of laugh lines radiating from eyes brown as tilled earth, and when she smiles Nona sees a row of natural teeth. One front tooth slightly overlaps the other, but this does not detract from her smile. Nona imagines that Chris is a woman who smiles often. A woman with lots of friends, even gentlemen friends. If she was, or *is*, a teacher, she would be the students' favourite. If a nurse, the one who took the time to listen to her patients, to really know them. Oh, of course any one of the other nurses was perfectly capable of checking their blood pressure or adjusting an IV drip, but it would be Chris's cheery voice they would listen for in the polished halls beyond their doors.

"I'm Nona." She doesn't feel the need to shake wet hands. Besides, if she lets go of the bar she'll start drifting, or her head will momentarily drop beneath the salty water, and she's been warned about taking it in the eyes.

"Nice to meet you."

A man with a sunken chest and a thicket of white hair between drooping nipples floats past their feet. An inflatable blue ring keeps his head out of the water. "I'd like to try that," Nona says.

"It's very relaxing."

Someone dives into the deep end and everyone looks to see who made the obnoxious smack. A man surfaces with one hand pinning his glasses to his nose.

Chris chuckles. "Some people — men especially — can't seem to resist calling attention to themselves, don't you think?"

"Yes," Nona says. "I suppose that's true."

They don't say anything for a long while. Two gentlemen idly drift past, large bellies breaking the water like minor icebergs. The room or the water itself affects sound here, so voices rise and fall in waves, are sensed more than heard. Like a record, Nona thinks, played at the wrong speed. She butts her head against the pool's edge and stretches out as far as she can — it feels so good! She listens to the water tingle, as if carbonated, and wipes a dry eyebrow, amazed that salt has collected even there.

"Well, I've had enough for now." Chris stands then, and pulls her bathing cap off. She's still mostly blonde, with grey streaks in thick bangs that fall across her forehead. She shakes her head and fluffs the back and sides of her hair. It's cut short but she has lots of it, Nona notes, bushels of it. Very early sixties, she guesses. Her cheekbones are high and prominent — quite striking. "Would you like to join me for dinner?"

"Dinner? I had my dinner," Nona says, "at noon."

"No, I mean supper. There's a pasta special tonight."

Oh. Another mistake. Chris probably doesn't eat until late either, Nona thinks, like Gerry's wife, who also calls supper "dinner." She can't wait that long. Now there's the hypoglycemia, but she's always had supper on the table by five. Even now, with Don gone, she likes to get her meal over with, her dishes done quickly so her evenings are free and clear. "That would be nice," she finds herself saying.

"Is seven okay?"

She'll have the cheese and crackers she'd stuffed into her purse. Perhaps a sandwich at the snack bar, if she needs it. "Seven is fine."

My, people are friendly, she thinks. This is a good place. She must send a note to Gerry, thanking him again.

❧❧❧

Chris is seated at a small, white-clothed table below a window when Nona arrives. She's been watching the door, and waves when Nona appears. The restaurant is almost full.

"I'm sorry," Nona begins. "Have you been waiting long?" A young waiter with spiked hair — all efficiency and likely expecting a good tip, she thinks — pulls her chair out and scoots it back in once she's seated. A little candle flickers in a red glass jar, and pink carnations lean against each other in a crystal vase.

"Just got here," Chris says. "Have you had a nice afternoon?"

"Quite. I had a massage and tootled around the gift shops a bit."

She parts her menu. It's a touch disconcerting to have to look someone in the eye — someone she doesn't really even know yet — when they are sitting so close together. She's never been good at it.

Chris, too, has opened her menu, the flaps resting in her palms like a hymnal. "I went for a long walk past the dance hall and back. It was a lovely day. Just enough wind to keep the air cool."

Nona looks out the window, taking in the valley scene. The rippling water, the late sun catching the tops of the gentle waves that push white foam and sludge onto the beach. Across the narrow lake the hills are tinted orange. It's mid September, a good day to harvest, she thinks. The busiest, most exasperating and thrilling weeks of their year. Except for taking meals to the field, it often seemed she didn't see Don for days on end, although of course he fell into bed beside her each night, hours after she'd already turned in, and was gone before first light. Sometimes the shape of him was all she had, the impression his solid body left on the white sheets. Sometimes, when she pressed her face into his pillow—his wind and wheat smell.

"What are you thinking about?" Chris asks.

Again, a question that gongs. "I, I was — "

"How long has he been gone?" Chris asks, tenderly.

"Two years, this October." Again to the window. The ice cream vendor across the street is closing his shutters. The days of vanilla and chocolate, double scooped on a cone, are fast coming to an end. Most of the tourists and those who will not be wintering in homes here — because you could hardly call some of these monstrosities cabins, Nona thinks — have left for the summer. "It was an aneurysm."

"I'm sorry."

Oh, what a thing, to be talking about her husband's death, now, when she's been invited out to have a nice time. No wonder her circle of friends is diminishing, like the rings of water left from a skipping stone; smaller, smaller, disappearing altogether.

The waiter returns. He calls them "girls" and takes their order, Chris's order, really. She seems to know how to pronounce things Nona has never heard of, and orders a glass of white wine by its real name. When it's Nona's turn, she says, "That sounds good. I'll have the same," not really knowing what will turn up.

"So, tell me about yourself," Chris is saying. She's folded the white linen napkin and placed it in her lap. "What do you keep busy at in Warman?"

"Well, I have friends, you know. And I play bridge. I like to watch my programs in the afternoon." It sounded so dull — so trivial and plain and grey — when it was out there like that. Even the walls here seem to have more life to them — more *of* a life — than she. Surely there was more. Her volunteering at the library, reading stories to toddlers. Her quilting. Don had been proud of that, had even called her an *artiste*. And she can ballroom dance. They'd taken lessons, and that's what she misses most. Not dancing. But of course she won't share that, she'll just let these thoughts dissolve like the afternoon light.

She wouldn't be surprised if Chris excused herself right after the meal. No, she would hang on until they'd had coffee and a sliver of pie, but she'll be racing to get away, Nona thinks. Suddenly she realizes that she hasn't even asked Chris much of anything about herself. Where does she live? What does she do? Or has she asked, and forgotten already?

"I'm sorry, but where did you say you live?" There, a way around it.

"I have two homes, really. I'm a psychologist, and my time is split between my research in Saskatoon and my practice in La Ronge. I do see quite a bit of the northern half of the province, actually. But I only keep an apartment there. I have a little house in the city, near the university. There's a suite in the basement, which I rent to students."

A psychologist! What would Don have made of that? And how can she be expected to go on with her unimportant little words now? "That sounds like interesting work," she manages to say. "Do you have a family?"

"No. I never married."

"Oh!"

"You sound surprised."

"Well . . . it's just — " Cripes. "I couldn't imagine living alone." Then, because she doesn't want it to sound like a criticism, she adds: "Having all that time to yourself, all that freedom to do as you please."

Chris smiles. "Well, I haven't been alone. Not *all* the time. And things have worked out. I'm not lonely, if that's what you're wondering. It's quite natural for people to think that a woman alone — in a restaurant, say, at a movie, or here, at the spa — is alone against her own choos — "She stops. "I'm sorry, I didn't mean to rant."

"Quite all right," Nona says, her load lifting a little now that Chris has shown a small fault. Nona digs into her pocket for her tablets — calcium and vitamin D — and discreetly swallows them with a sip of tepid water.

They eat then, and Nona is pleased with the meal, though she fears the garlic will give her some trouble. She has a second glass of wine; an extravagance. When did they ever drink wine at home?

The waiter brings the bill. Nona pulls her purse off the floor and retrieves her wallet.

"No, please," Chris touches two fingers to Nona's wrist. "I invited you."

"Well, I didn't expect to — "

"Please, Nona," she says, firmly, but not without kindness. "I insist."

"All right then," she says, closing the gold clasp. But now she is indebted, and that won't do. Perhaps she'll find a little something at one of the gift shops and drop it at Chris's room. She cannot leave it at this.

"I'm afraid I must be going. My son — in Nanaimo — he's expecting me to call tonight. This was lovely. Thank you." She is out of her chair and through the door in a snap.

Why had she said that? It isn't true, and it is not at all like her to lie. It had been an enjoyable meal and a pleasing hour, even if Chris *is* a psychologist. She hadn't lorded it over Nona in any way. She hadn't tried to pick her brains apart.

"Silly old gal," Nona chides herself, back in her room. She sits on the firm bed and lets the shoes drop off her feet.

The bed is dressed in a sea green spread; a foreign colour, to Nona's Prairie eyes. In the corner there's a dark walnut dresser with a handsome oval mirror, and a television that Nona has not yet turned on. Above the bed an almost colourless painting of a Victorian girl feeding ducks.

She wishes — not for any practical reason — that there were a calendar on the wall. At home, on the farm, they had a calendar tacked up in every room. Don used to bring them home from the crop insurance agent, the Wheat Pool, the Co-op, the Credit Union and the drugstore, and she'd go about pinning them up, never forgetting to flip the months. She tries to recall the final ones, before they started stripping the house down, getting it ready for sale. The kitchen calendar by the telephone, with the birthdays and anniversaries of community people printed into the squares. She no longer has one like that, does not want to be reminded that for her and Don there will be no more anniversaries, never another boiled raisin cake on his birthday. On the porch, where Don hung his coveralls and washed the dirt and grease off his hands before coming any further into the house, a calendar with different types of machinery — a swather, a disker, a combine — on each page. Their bedroom calendar featured scenes from provincial parks they never visited, and in the bathroom — oh, what was it in her pretty lilac bathroom? — oh yes, twelve glossy paintings by the Masters. That one was from Jodie, their daughter-in-law; Don had scoffed at it. But here, no calendar. Just the small card she keeps in her wallet, if she really must know the date.

"I'm exhausted," she says to the calendar-free walls. "I'll just have a little nap now. Not even all the way under, just pull the quilt over my legs.

That's it. Just a rest."

శుశుశు

There is so much to look at Nona hardly knows where to begin. Racks and racks of fancy bathing suits; framed etchings of farm buildings sinking back into the land; delicate blown glass bottles; wheat-weaved and hand-sewn floppy-legged dolls, the latter in large bonnets and aprons; hand-made cards with photographs or dried flowers and no verses inside; a wall display of cassette tapes where, if you pushed a button, you could sample their sounds. She is standing in front of this display, wondering about "Sea Birds," when she feels a hand light on her shoulder.

"Hello, Nona."

"Hello, Chris." Nona wishes she could hide the burgundy beeswax candles: her gift, found out.

"Are you buying a tape?"

"No . . . well, maybe. There's so much to choose from."

Chris pushes the button for "Spring Brook." The sounds of trickling water and soft organ music — no, not organ, some instrument that Nona has likely never heard of — emanate from hidden speakers.

"I love the sound of water," Chris says. "I have a little waterfall in my back yard, in the city. Whenever I can, I eat lunch on the patio and watch the birds bathe. Do you enjoy bird-watching?"

"Well, yes. I especially love their sounds. I used to walk down our sun-dappled lane as I went for the mail and count all the different songs I heard." She closes her eyes, remembering that sweetness.

"That's very poetic."

"Oh. Well. I don't know, but it was something I enjoyed." She moves past the cassettes and fingers a basket of thimbles with prairie lilies painted on them. "I'd like to buy you something, I mean for the meal last night. Is there anything in particular you'd like?"

Chris turns from a display of handmade earrings."Nona, that meal last night was my pleasure. You certainly don't have to reciprocate with a gift."

"But I — "

Two couples shuffle into the gift shop in terry bathrobes and Birkenstock sandals. One woman's hair is pulled back into the shape of a cinnamon bun, or a danish. The taller man points out various objects and explains the significance of the local trinkets in German. His hairless toes hang over his sandals like claws. When he stops explaining and sees Chris in her long denim dress, he pauses, and nods hello. Maybe she hasn't noticed, Nona thinks. Attractive people likely get attention all the time.

"I'm going in for my soak now," Chris says. "Would you like to join me?"

"Perhaps later. I have a little more browsing to do."

"All right, then." Chris touches Nona's arm and says goodbye.

"Goodbye," Nona says, watching her new friend go. The Germans watch her, too.

ৼৢৼৢৼৢ

There are many more people in the spa this afternoon. Nona pads barefoot across the deck — she's forgotten her thongs — with the large white spa towel tucked beneath her folded arms. The pool is a hushed sea of floating bodies; movements made as if in slow motion. The whole world slowed down. A time warp, Nona thinks, where chronic pain and tension are miraculously melted away.

Some of the aged bathers float on their fronts, clutching beach balls beneath their chests; others are slow-moving continents of skin floating on their backs. Still others anchor themselves by gripping the rails, eyes closed, or open to the sweating cedar beams high above. A one-armed man with the skin below his elbow smoothed into a tuck sports the unmistakable reddened face and neck of a farmer. He sits on the pool's edge, slowly stirring the water with his feet. Except for the arm, Nona thinks, it could be Don. The broad shoulders, high forehead and hair the colour of ash, white where it's clipped neatly above his ears. Not fair, she thinks. But of course he's really nothing like Don at all. Don didn't like the water.

One lounge chair is unclaimed. She drapes her towel across it and scans the water for Chris's yellow bathing cap. Not there. She steps into the largest area of the divided pool, where it is cooler but still a comfort, like a bathtub left a few minutes too long. She bobs forward, a moon walker, until she's up to her neck in it. Nona has never learned to swim, but it is impossible to sink in the relaxing water, and the lure of adventure — felt as a vague popping between her breasts — drives her further. She lifts the rope and dips beneath, toward the deep end, and for the first time in her sixty-seven years, she is free, weightless, swimming.

❧❧❧❧

Nona sees the poster in the women's change room — an advertisement for tonight's event at Danceland, the colossal, ancient pavilion on the east beach with the intricate arched roof and springy, horsehair floor. Where Chris had gone for her walk. "For more than seventy years,"

Nona reads, "dancers from across the Prairies have been flocking to Danceland to enjoy all styles of music, from big band to old time. Come join the fun!"

Perhaps she will walk over and have a look this afternoon. The exercise would do her back good, and it would be nice to get out to enjoy the sun. She is still in her wet bathing suit, the salt drying on her skin and in her hair. She wipes flakes off her arm, clutches a thin bunch of hair at the back of her head and hears it crackle. Goodness! She steps beneath a showerhead and rinses her hair, then squirts soap from the dispenser and works it into her arms. Good arms, she thinks, the forearms still strong, the skin only a little looser in the two years she's been in town. That's how she's learning to word it now. Not "since Don died," but "since I moved to town." She has slips. She soaps an underarm, eyes closed beneath the stream.

"Hello, Nona." That voice. Soothing, as if it, too, has been washed in the warm, healing water.

"Chris. I didn't see you in the pool."

Chris steps beneath the shower across from Nona. "No bathing cap today," she says, "I forgot it. I must have looked like anyone else out there."

But how could that be true? Nona wondered. How many others would peel out of their suits and take the public shower straight to their skin? When she realizes she's staring, Nona averts her attention and squeezes conditioner into her hair. Of course Chris could do that. She still has the high, small breasts of a much younger woman. A girl. And she hasn't had children, so she doesn't carry a purse of old skin around her front, like Nona, who steps out of the shower spray and reaches for her towel.

She enters a cubicle, one hand holding the too-narrow curtain closed while the other awkwardly pushes her suit over her hips. Chris brushes past in her towel. "Did you see the poster?"

Dried and dressed, Nona gathers her things and moves to the large change room mirror. "Yes. I suppose it's a big attraction, with the horsehair floor. I may go have a look this afternoon."

"Would you like to go to the dance?"

Nona can't help herself, she laughs. "I don't think I could. I mean, if there were a bunch, maybe, but just the two of us — " She lets it hang there. Remembers her niece's wedding, in June. Nona knows the wall now, what it's like to sit at a table alone when an especially good song is played and all the others get up with their partners, leaving her to fiddle with her napkin or pretend she's searching for something in her purse for ten minutes. Times when moments are dragged by slow horses. Certainly there were those — relatives and Gerry's friends, elbowed into it by their wives—who'd given her a spin around the floor, but it was staged, and none of them, though they did try their best, really knew how to dance.

"Oh, come on. It'll be fun. And the dance hall is quite famous, actually." Chris is dressed now, in navy slacks and a sharp blouse with a pattern of black triangles, a small gold chain. She takes up a spot in the mirror beside Nona. "People have been enjoying concerts and dances out here since before you and I were born. You really should experience it — "

Nona drives back tomorrow. She'll call Gerry and Jodie, and her daughter-in-law will want to know every detail. Did she go for the pedicure? Did she have the reflexology treatment? How was it? And what about the famous dance hall? Had she walked across it, felt it move beneath her feet? "All right then. As long as I don't have to dress up too much. I haven't brought anything fancy along."

"Good for you," Chris says. "Good for you, Nona."

જ્ઞ

How it happens is the orchestra plays a waltz and it's not even anything Nona recognizes but the violin, the violin she knows in her throat. It turns her heart over, hard. The group at their table — up now with the music — is a loud, joking bunch of retired business people. Golfers, getting in their eighteen holes a day. After the initial small talk there hadn't been much to say.

Chris has been looking at her apologetically all evening. "Would you like to leave?"

Nona is staring. The dance floor is a pastel sweep of fabric as women are twirled, their wide skirts dusting against each other like the wings of moths at the yard light. Beneath them the floor is undulating, everything in motion, everything brighter there beneath the white, paper-covered lights than in the dusk that swallows the sidelines. "Not yet," she says, and then she does something she will re-experience three times a day as long as she lives. She pulls Chris off her chair and onto the floor, her hand between her friend's shoulders as they join the music and the dance, two soft, warm bodies holding steady against the unsinkable night.

SHELLEY A. LEEDAHL was born in Kyle,
Saskatchewan, in 1963. She writes novels,
poetry, nonfiction and children's literature as
well as short stories, and frequently conducts
author visits in schools and libraries across the
country. In 2002/2003, she was a participant
in the Canada-Mexico Writing/Photography
Exchange in Mérida, Mexico and Banff, Canada.
In 2004, she was awarded a Fellowship to
attend the Hawthornden Castle International
Retreat for Writers, near Edinburgh, Scotland.
She lives in Saskatoon and Middle Lake,
Saskatchewan.